RESISTING ROSE

TARA GRACE ERICSON

SILVER FOUNTAIN PRESS

Cover Models: Matt and Deana Coufal
Cover Photo: Emily Kowalski Photography
Cover by Cat's Pyjamas Design

Paperback ISBN-13: 978-1-949896-20-6
Ebook ISBN-13: 978-1-949896-21-3

For my husband.
I am so blessed to have married my best friend.

"For it is God who works in you, both to will and to work for his good pleasure."

Philippians 2.13

CONTENTS

PROLOGUE

*L*aura Bloom sipped her coffee and studied the bulletin board hanging in the corner of her bedroom. Nearly every morning for the last twenty years had been welcomed with a pocket of time in this chair, spending precious moments with the Lord and praying for her family.

Over the past five years, the contents of the bulletin board had shifted to accommodate the additions to their family, including her grandchildren. Five of her seven children had found their life partner, and each had been married right here on the family farm.

Lavender and Emmett had gotten married two years ago, and Laura said a quick prayer for guidance for their next steps. Emmett's books were still extremely successful and Lavender's own devotional for young women had led to a speaking tour around the country.

Her eyes landed on a photo of Lily and Josh from their intimate wedding celebration three years ago. Seeing the change in her eldest daughter had been the reward for years of persistent prayer. Lily had finally let go of the wounds of her past and embraced the forgiveness and joy of salvation. It was all her mother ever wanted.

An old photo of Dandelion in her Army fatigues brought another wave of longing and one of joyous expectation. Andi would finally return home next year after retiring from the military. It had been decades since her daughter had lived nearby.

Laura's fervent desire was that the farm would always be here for her children to come home to. Poppy and Harrison split their time between their newly built home on the parcel of the farm and Indianapolis, where Harrison was entering his third year of the governorship. Hawthorne and Avery had built a house on the farm as well. Avery still worked in Terre Haute at the university and Hawthorne had taken over most of the management responsibilities on the farm, leaving her and Keith to enjoy slower days and more travel. She said another prayer of thanks for how Keith had healed from his stroke five years prior.

Last, her eyes landed on a photo of Rose. Her youngest daughter had a tender heart, though she was tough as nails when she set her mind to something. Rose loved the animals of the farm, and Laura knew nothing could tear her away from her responsibility to them. Between Hawthorne, Rose, and their produce operation manager, Tate, Bloom's Farm was in good hands.

Tate had been there for four years and proven himself hardworking and loyal. He was a good friend to Rose. Sometimes she wondered if there could be something more between them. Laura prayed for Rose's work, faith, and future. Then she prayed the same for Tate, who'd become part of the family over the past few years. She might not be his mother, but Tate was far from home and something was preventing him from going back.

1

Tate showed the college student how to water the seedlings with the gentle misters hanging near soil level in the greenhouse. The tiny tomato plants would be transplanted in May, still months away. There was still plenty of work to be done before then. The greenhouse was the center of all the farm activity on these cold February days. The heated building was the key to a productive growing season when the Indiana weather warmed up in the spring.

He let his employee take over and glanced around the building. He'd held a lot of jobs in the decade since he left home, and the difference between his family's ranch in Montana and the hybrid family farm in Indiana had been interesting.

He didn't know much about growing crops when he started. Poppy Bloom had been a good teacher, along with Hawthorne, who was technically his boss.

As though summoned by the thought, the door to the greenhouse swung open and Hawthorne ducked inside. Tate felt the cold blast of air wash through the building and watched Hawthorne stomp the snow from his boots. Hawthorne removed his stocking cap. "Ah, it feels good in here."

"A balmy 60 degrees for our little sprouts. How's it going?"

Hawthorne shrugged. "Heater on the goat trough is on the fritz, so I was down there looking at it."

Tate nodded his head. Been there, but with cattle back in Montana. Keeping the water from freezing could become its own full-time job if the equipment didn't cooperate.

"Rose said to tell you that Margie is getting close to kidding and to leave your phone on tonight."

The goat had been close for what seemed like weeks, but he just nodded. Helping Rose with the animals wasn't exactly in his job description, but he didn't mind. Rose did most of the work anyway, with her vet tech experience combined with her years growing up on the farm. It would be a lot more convenient if animals didn't almost always insist on the middle of the night to deliver their babies.

"Anything else?"

Hawthorne glanced back at the door with a groan. "My toes are barely thawed. Surely you've got a job for me in here."

Tate looked around the greenhouse at the handful of employees packing soil blocks and seeding. When the flats full of tiny onions and celery were full, they would slide neatly into the racks with high intensity lights to help them grow.

"I do have a bank of lights that isn't working. I was going to take a look at it, but you are welcome to handle it instead. I'm guessing it's just a fuse."

Hawthorne clapped his hands together, still covered with the padded winter gloves. "Perfect. I'll take a look."

Tate felt his phone vibrate with a text message. He pointed Hawthorne to the broken unit of lights before checking the screen.

RB: Tonight's the night. I'm almost positive. I'll bring the coffee this time.

TR: Are you *kidding* me? (pun intended)

He could almost picture Rose rolling her eyes at him and he chuckled. Then quickly sent another message.

TR: I'll be there.

It would make tomorrow an especially long day, but there was something incredible about seeing an animal being brought into the world. No matter how many times he saw it, he would never tire of seeing how God had created everything to work so naturally.

He still sometimes wished he'd been able to take over the livestock operation instead. Rose had proven remarkably stubborn in that regard.

He smiled, remembering the first time she'd caught him in her barn. She'd immediately been defensive, with a snarky tone and lots of questions, but when their mutual love of the animals had become obvious, she warmed up to the newcomer. That had been four years ago, and now Rose was probably his closest friend in the world. Between living at the farm in his trailer and working there, he didn't have a lot of friends. Hawthorne was quite a bit older than Tate and busy with his wife, Avery. The solitude didn't bother Tate. The less he talked to people, the fewer questions he had to answer. Everyone was always curious about why he'd left Montana, which he'd rather not talk about.

Even Rose didn't really know the whole story. She was his closest friend in the world, but his past was better left untouched. Besides, how could Rose understand? Her family was the epitome of love and affection. His on the other hand? Not even close.

HE TUCKED his phone back into the pocket of his jeans and shrugged into his brown Carhartt coat. "I'm headed to my office. Call me if you need anything." His office was tucked in the corner of the large barn that served as the base for the produce operation and housed their tractors, seeds, and staging ground for sales. He dreaded the paperwork, but now was the most critical time for tracking the number of community-supported agriculture, or CSA, basket subscribers. He also had to carefully plan and manage the schedule and real estate for the greenhouse and the fields for the next six months. Poppy had left efficient systems in place, but as the programs grew, it was up to him to adjust. If things continued like they were, he might consider proposing an additional greenhouse.

It felt good to be trusted to make suggestions. His opinion was respected at Bloom's Farm in a way it never had been at home. Another reason he was tempted to stick around longer than he thought he would.

~

ROSE SPREAD the pig feed around the pen so Tank, the largest male, wouldn't eat more than his fair share before the others had a chance. In the pen with the females, she did the same. The piglets were still nursing, but they were starting to eat the feed as well.

Rose checked their water and carefully stepped through the gate before closing it behind her. Her breath formed clouds in front of her in the frigid air, and the two layers of wool socks didn't help nearly enough with keeping her toes warm in the muck boots she wore.

She stopped by Margie's enclosure again and saw the mother goat pacing gently. She'd been on the verge of kidding for days, but tonight was definitely the night. Rose grinned in anticipation. The petting zoo visitors this summer would love the new additions. Rose lifted her arms over her head and stretched. She'd already been working for nearly five hours, and it was only noon. If tonight was slated to be as late as she suspected, a nap this afternoon might be in order.

Unsurprisingly, there was too much to do and not enough time. In the cold February days, taking care of the animals wasn't for the faint of heart. She loved it though. Growing up on Bloom's Farm, helping her father with the animals and the crops, she'd developed a deep love for it. Being trained as a veterinary technician had been a logical decision for her. Her schooling gave her an extra level of confidence when making decisions and caring for the livestock. Unfortunately, it seemed no matter how much time she spent caring for the animals, her family would always view her as little Rosie, the baby of the family who needed to be coddled and supervised.

She caught a glimpse of her father near the edge of the barn and rolled her eyes. There he was again, supervising her. Rose tamped down the frustration and lifted a hand in greeting.

Keith walked toward her with a smile. "Hey, Rosie. How's Margie looking?"

"She's close. It's got to be tonight. How are you doing?" She'd never look at her father the same way she used to. She scanned his face for signs of fatigue and took a step closer in case he needed a steadying arm.

He smiled. "I'm doing great, Rosie. Don't you worry. Mind if I take a look at Margie, too?"

Rose smiled tightly. "Sure thing." Of course, her dad wanted to check himself, as though she hadn't handled dozens of kiddings in the last three years alone. She loved him deeply, but sometimes she just wanted her dad to see her as capable.

"You're right, she's already in the early stages. Do you need Hawthorne to help tonight?"

Rose shook her head. "No, but thanks. Tate and I will be out here in case she needs anything." She immediately regretted including Tate's presence in that statement. If he couldn't come, she would have been fine on her own.

Keith nodded. "Sounds good." Rose couldn't help but wonder if he would have pushed Hawthorne on her if Tate wasn't around. Did he trust everyone more than her? Her dad walked away and Rose brushed the hair from her face and sniffled from the cold air. It didn't matter. She was a Bloom, and this was her farm.

*L*ater that afternoon, Rose frowned at the text message from her sister Daisy.

DB: Family meeting at Storybook in thirty minutes.

Why did they need a family meeting, and why was it at Storybook Barn? Possibilities swirled through her thoughts. Was something wrong with Lily? Had her cancer returned? Four years ago, Lily was diagnosed and treated for stage one uterine cancer but had since been declared cancer free.

When Rose parked in front of Storybook Barn twenty-five minutes later, it wasn't the meeting she was expecting. The event center was perched on a large hill near the farm entrance, and the view overlooked the sprawling pastures and fields of

Bloom's Farm. Her family members stood at the edge of the parking lot, and the sun glinted brilliantly off the pristine snow blanketing the hillside below.

"What's going on, Daze?" Rose didn't wait to ask. The rest of the family looked as clueless as she was.

"Hold up. Still waiting for Tate and the crew."

Rose frowned. Wasn't this a family meeting? Sure, Tate had been around for a long time. But he wasn't family. And the rest of the crew was even more confusing.

Tate pulled in with a truckload of his workers and climbed down from his truck. "We're here. What did you need help moving?"

Daisy laughed joyfully. "There's nothing to move and no family meeting."

"Then can I get back to work?" Lily's no-nonsense tone dimmed Daisy's smile a fraction.

"No." Daisy opened the trunk of her car and pulled out something large and colorful.

"Are those—"

"Sleds!" Daisy exclaimed. "The snow is going to start melting tomorrow and everybody needs to let loose a little bit."

"This is ridiculous, even for you, Daisy." There

was Lily again, ever practical. "Aren't we too old for this?"

Hawthorne grabbed a sled and pushed it into Tate's arms, "Race you to the bottom!"

Rose grinned as her brother took off running toward the hill.

Tate looked around blankly for a second, then shrugged before racing after his boss. Rose's mouth fell open as the two men extended the round plastic sleds out in front of themselves and leapt into the air, landing on the discs and sliding down the hill on their stomachs like penguins.

She shook her head at their antics, but their yells of excitement as they neared the bottom had her considering a run of her own. While Hawthorne and Tate high-fived and trudged back up the hill, three of the college students who worked in the greenhouse embraced the activity and headed down the hill.

Rose stepped next to Daisy who was watching proudly. "What inspired this little impromptu field day?"

Daisy grinned. "The sleds were on sale for three bucks a piece. I figured it was high time we gave the staff a little taste of the fun side of Bloom's Farm."

Rose remembered hours spent on this hill when they were kids, sliding down and traipsing back up to do it all over again. They went until they were wet and exhausted, then greeted back home by warm mugs of cocoa.

Rose grinned. "You should tell Mom and Dad to come watch. They'd probably get a kick out of it."

"You're totally right." Daisy stepped away to call their parents.

Tate and Hawthorne had reached the top of the hill, and she laughed at how out of breath they were.

Hawthorne sat on the parking block and huffed. "I feel like going down that hill was a lot shorter than it used to be, and climbing up it was a lot farther."

Tate slapped him on the shoulder. "Come on, it wasn't that bad."

It was no secret that Hawthorne loved having another guy around the farm. Growing up with six sisters, he'd been outnumbered pretty much his entire life. And Tate fit in perfectly. She remembered her own fears when he first arrived. He had years of experience in ranching, and though Tate had been hired to handle the produce operation, she'd been terrified that he would encroach on her territory.

Those fears turned out to be unfounded though. Tate had showed interest in the livestock, but remained solidly dedicated to his responsibility with the crops and the orchard. He turned to look at Rose. "Guess this old man needs a breather. Are you up for it, Rose? Or are you scared you'll lose?"

She raised an eyebrow. "Is that a challenge?"

"I smell a wager," Hawthorne commented from his place on the ground.

Tate shrugged. "I'll bet chicken coop duty that I can beat you down the hill."

Rose shook her head. "No bet. You weigh more than me. You'll go faster." She grabbed the sled from Hawthorne and grinned. "Points for style and speed."

"Deal. If you win, I'll clean the chicken coop. If I win, you have to help me with inventory next week."

Rose considered the stakes. There was nothing worse than mindlessly counting seedlings and fertilizer bags. She looked at the sled in her hands, rubbing rough blue plastic with her fingertips.

"Fine. But Lily is the judge."

"Works for me."

"Nobody asked me," Lily commented dryly.

"You can go down the hill if you'd rather?" Rose said with a chuckle. There was no way Lily would be sledding, and everyone there knew it.

"Fine. I'll judge."

Tate offered to let her go first, but she waved him

forward. She didn't want him to see what she had up her sleeve. He sauntered up to the edge of the hill then turned back toward everyone. He saluted with one hand and then leaned backward, landing on the sled and careening down the hill with a goofy grin on his face.

Rose smiled at her friend's routine. Not too shabby. But she wouldn't lose. Doing inventory was not an option. Tate slowed to a stop at the base of the hill and stood up, raising his arms overhead in triumph. Rose shook her finger at him. "Not so fast, Cowboy," she said to herself as she stepped up to the edge.

Rose leaned over and placed her hands on the sled, then kicked her legs to one side, launching herself down the hill into a continuous rotation. She balanced on her knees as she spun around and around, speeding quickly down the hill. With each rotation, she saw Tate getting closer, and she laughed gaily as he jumped out of the way. She soon came to a stop and sat still for a moment to gather her balance before standing up and taking a bow.

She could hear cheers from the top of the hill. Tate smiled broadly. "Okay, Flowers. That was pretty good."

"Don't sound so surprised." She glanced up the

hill. It did look bigger than she remembered. "Let's go see what Lily has to say. But just so I don't forget… the chicken coop is due to be cleaned on Tuesday." Rose laughed at his pained expression and started her trek up the hillside.

TATE FOLLOWED Rose up the hill. He knew Lily would officially announce him as the loser, but he couldn't seem to mind. It was worth it to see Rose laughing as she flew down the hill. She definitely wasn't afraid of a challenge. Though she took her work seriously, Rose was always one to lighten the mood with a joke, usually at Hawthorne's expense.

This afternoon hadn't been what he'd expected. Daisy's message had made it seem like they needed help moving chairs and tables at Storybook Barn. As he watched the college students he employed sledding down the hill and attempting to crash into one another, he was glad Daisy had interrupted.

He knew as well as anyone that the long winter months could be dreary and depressing. His team had been working hard, packing planting blocks and carefully inserting seeds for the last week or two. Before that, it had been a marathon of deep cleaning and organization to get everything ready for the season. His team deserved a break.

In fact, they all did.

It was things like this—the family gatherings, the fun and games—that made Bloom's Farm worlds away from the ranch he grew up on. At Russell Ranch, it had been all work and no play. Especially after his mother had died. Fun was a luxury that Steve Russell had no time for.

They reached the top of the hill with little conversation and he looked hopefully at Lily.

"Tate, I gave you an 8.5 for creativity and speed. You were faster than Rose, and going backward was a nice touch." Lily turned to Rose. "Rose, I gave you a... 9.0. Daisy counted six full rotations on the way down, and you got extra points for almost running Tate over."

"Hey!" he blurted out with mock offense.

"Sorry, Cowboy," Rose teased. "Better luck next time."

"Double or nothing?"

She laughed but shook her head. "No way."

The sledding continued around them. Poppy had arrived with the kids and she watched nervously as Hawthorne took Magnolia with him on her first ride. Rose pulled down the tailgate of Tate's truck and hopped up. He took a seat next to her and watched Daisy convince Poppy to go down the hill with her.

"You still coming tonight?" Rose's question broke the silence between them and he nodded.

"Wouldn't miss it."

"It's okay if you need to. I can handle it." Her expression was serious.

Tate shook his head once. "Never said you couldn't. I like being there though." He knew Rose was more than capable. Who was she trying to convince?

"Okay. It's nice to have the company." Her tone didn't quite match her words, and he laughed at the seriousness in her voice.

"Come on, Flowers. You're going to make me blush with all that sweet talk."

Rose's solemn expression broke into a smile, and she leaned over to nudge his shoulder. "Don't go getting a big head. It'll be a long night. I'll bring the coffee."

3

Rose peeked into Margie's pen from around the corner, trying not to disturb the laboring animal. The goat was breathing heavily and making low moaning sounds. It wouldn't be long.

She felt the warmth of Tate standing next to her, and the piney trace of his soap tickled her nose. He whispered, "Hey, how's she doing?"

She turned and led them back down the hall toward the offices. "She's doing great. She's been laboring for a bit, but I want to give her a little more time to try on her own before I go interfere. Cup of coffee?" She held up the large green steel thermos.

Tate nodded. "Anything warm is welcome at this point."

"Could be worse. At least the snow is melting." She poured them each a mug of the coffee she'd brought with her from the main house.

"Oh yeah. I'd much rather have mud four inches deep," he said sarcastically.

Rose chuckled at his attitude. "I'll remind you of that when we get another foot of snow."

He gave a dramatic tremor of disgust.

"What are the winters like in Montana?" Rose watched his eyes quickly fall to the mug in his hands at her question. Tate didn't talk about home very much, but Rose was fascinated by the stories he let slip about the ranch where he'd grown up.

"Not too different from here. Mostly cold and snowy, though sometimes the Chinook winds would bring a warm snap to keep it interesting: keeping the cattle safe during a rough blizzard or driving the truck out to drop hay in the pasture when it was fifteen below. You know how it is."

Rose nodded. She did know, even though they didn't have hundreds of head of cattle. She could keep her little herd of cows relatively close to the barn during the winter. The goats, sheep, and hogs had pens that were semi-enclosed, and the animals could come inside during the worst of the weather. The horses had stalls that opened to a corral with a pasture beyond. And the chickens? They had a coop but mostly ran around wherever.

"Should we go check on Margie?" Tate's question interrupted Rose's thoughts about the animals and the logistics of increasing her herd sizes for any of them.

She set down the empty coffee cup and stood. "Yeah, let's check her out."

Margie's low moaning sounded rough and Rose approached slowly as Tate followed. "Hey there, girl. How are you doing?" She shushed the laboring mother and held out her hands slowly. "It's okay. Just let me take a little look, all right?" Rose continued talking to the tired animal as she laid her hands gently on the goat's side.

TATE WATCHED as Rose comforted the scared animal. Her gentle tone and confident nature soothed the mother, and he felt a surge of admiration for his friend. Rose checked the progress and grinned back at him. "Just a few more pushes."

She urged the animal on and then took hold of the kid's hooves to help extract the animal. With a laugh of joy, Rose cleared the airway of the new kid.

Tate handed her a stack of towels to dry it off. Almost immediately, the kid wobbled up onto its legs and nestled closer to its mother.

Tate felt the wide smile on his face as the mama goat licked the baby's face. Rose's hands went back to the goat's side. "Looks like you've got twins, Margie." A few minutes later, Rose's smile dropped, and she turned to him. "The second baby is upside down."

"What can I do?"

Margie moaned, and Rose stroked the goat's side before turning back to him. "There's a box of gloves over there. Can you grab it?"

He found the gloves and obediently brought it to Rose. Her voice lilted over soft words. "It's okay, mama. We're going to get this baby out, okay? You can do this. We can do this."

Rose removed her coat and grabbed a plastic glove, pulling it up past her elbow. "Okay, sweetie. This isn't going to feel good, but it's our only option."

Tate flinched as Rose confidently reached in and slowly rotated the baby goat inside of Margie. He watched Rose's face instead of the procedure. Her face was a solemn mask of concentration. She closed her eyes and the barn was eerily silent except for the labored moaning of Margie and the mewling noises of the healthy kid. When Rose relaxed, Tate realized she had removed her hand.

"Got it," she proclaimed with a grin.

Tate watched as Rose assisted Margie with the rest of the labor, the exhausted mother goat barely able to push. When the second kid emerged, Tate caught Rose's proud smile. Despite the chill in the air, her face was warm and flushed.

"There we go, little one." He cleaned up the baby goat and watched it totter over to its mother, looking for milk.

While Rose cleaned herself up, Tate raked up the soiled bedding and laid out fresh straw doing his best to not disturb the new family. He watched from the edge of the enclosure, and Rose came up behind him. "Have you done that before?"

Rose shrugged. "I did it once when I worked for the vet. Sometimes I'll have to reach in because only one leg is extended, or because the neck is back. That's the worst one if you don't catch it in time. There's nothing worse than a stillborn." He could hear the sadness in her voice. Her compassion for the animals was unmatched by anyone he'd ever met before. Since he'd been helping, they hadn't had a stillborn, but he could imagine the heartbreak that would bring.

He held open her coat, which he had rescued from the floor of the pen where she discarded it. While Rose slipped her arms into it, his fingers brushed her shoulders. Tate tried to come up with a response. "Well, either way, that was pretty amazing."

She turned to him and smiled. He could see the circles under her green eyes, but they sparkled with the excitement of a successful kidding. His fingers twitched with the desire to touch her again. "We make a pretty good team, I'd say."

His heart flipped inside his chest, and he swallowed heavily. Rose was his friend. Why was he reading more into those words than he should? "Yeah," he choked out. "A great team."

Her smile broadened, and he felt his resolve tumble a little further. He'd known for years that she was passionate and funny and tough and gorgeous. So why was he suddenly imagining what it would be like to kiss her? Tate realized he'd been staring and cleared his throat, shifting his weight as he looked toward Margie and back again.

Her hand flew to her mouth to stifle a yawn, and Tate checked his watched. Three in the morning. "We better get some sleep."

Rose nodded. "I just have to make sure the kids

are nursing okay." No surprises there. Rose would always put the animals' needs before her own, and arguing with her wouldn't make any difference. He'd learned that from experience. He followed her as she approached the newborns and double checked they were receiving milk from the clearly tired, but preening Margie.

He patted her head. "Great job, Margie. Such a good mama," he said gently.

Rose stood back up but stumbled. Tate held out his arms to steady her, and Rose sagged slightly before straightening. "Must sleep." Now that the adrenaline from delivery was wearing off, Rose must be exhausted.

He hit the remote start on his truck and heard it roar to life outside. He held her arm as they walked out of the barn. "Come on. I'll give you a lift back to the house."

Rose shook her head. "I can walk. It's not far."

"Rose, it's two degrees out here. And you can barely walk straight. I've got to drive to the trailer anyway."

She yawned again. "Okay, fine. If you insist."

She was adorable when she was sleepy. It was perhaps his favorite part of their middle-of-the-night tradition. When she'd first invited him three years ago, he'd come more out of interest. Cows were different from goats, after all. Since then, he'd come for nearly every calf, kid, and litter of piglets that had been born.

The truck heater was roaring when they climbed inside, and he heard Rose's contented sigh as she held her hands in front of the vents. She reached over and flipped on the heated seat. Tate couldn't stand the things, but every time Rose was in his truck, she turned hers on.

When she opened her mouth, Tate knew exactly what she was going to say. It was the same comment she made every time she rode in his truck. "I need to get me a truck like this," he said in unison with her.

She gave him an incredulous look before bursting into laughter. He winked at her, which only made her laugh harder. Somebody was a little slap happy.

The drive to the main house took less than two minutes, and Tate drove as slowly as he could, reluctant to end the evening. Rose was still laughing. She looked so dang gorgeous with her messy hair peeking out from under her stocking cap.

He pulled into the circle drive and Rose gave him one last grin. "Thanks for keeping me company."

"Anytime, Flowers. See you tomorrow."

Rose jumped down from the cab and jogged inside, his headlights illuminating her path. Once she was safely inside the house, Tate released the brake and slowly rolled away from the house. His lonely trailer parked near the edge of the property seemed especially uninviting after an evening spent with Rose.

4

*T*hree hours of sleep wasn't nearly enough, but Rose silenced her alarm and sat up in bed. While Daisy was known to set fourteen alarms to wake herself up, Rose had only ever needed one. Once you were awake, what was the point of an extra four minutes? Plus, this morning, she knew the baby goats were waiting to greet her. That was worth getting out of bed.

When she got to the barn, Tate's truck was parked outside. She smiled. Apparently, he couldn't wait to see them again either. Rose stepped inside and looked longingly toward the office where the coffeepot was waiting. Instead, she walked the other direction toward the small kidding pen where Margie and the baby goats would be waiting.

Tate turned as she approached, a mug in his hands. "Good morning," he said with a crooked smile.

In lieu of a greeting, she grabbed the mug from his hands and took a sip.

"Help yourself," he said wryly.

"Thanks." She gestured toward the goats. "How're they doing?"

"Everything looks good. Margie is a trooper. Have you named the kids yet?"

She shook her head. "Any ideas?"

Tate pulled the cup from her hand and raised it to his lips. Rose tried not to follow the path with her eyes. "One boy and one girl, right?" After she confirmed, he continued. "How about Harry and Sally?"

She tipped her head back with a laugh. "Yeah, all right."

They watched the babies jump around the small enclosure while Margie munched contentedly at the feed trough hung on the wall.

"Will they join the rest today?"

Rose nodded in response, then glanced at her watch. "Yeah. I better get to it."

"Need any help?"

Tate's offer warmed Rose from her toes to her

hat. Why was it when Hawthorne or her dad offered to help, she immediately felt insulted and inadequate, but when Tate offered, she felt cared for?

Still, she didn't need his help. He had his own work to do, anyway. "No, but thanks for the offer."

Tate's fingers touched the brim of his baseball cap and he tipped it slightly. "All right then. I'll see you around."

He turned to go, and Rose stopped him with a hand on his arm. "Wait."

Tate glanced back, expectantly. With a grin, Rose grabbed the mug from him and took one last drink. "You make good coffee, Cowboy."

He gave an exaggerated pout and looked down at the lidded cup. "Yeah, I know. I usually like to drink it myself." Then he met her eyes again. "Of course, if you are usually drinking the swill Hawthorne makes, I can't really blame you for stealing mine."

Rose chuckled at the dig aimed at her brother and watched Tate walk away. He lifted the coffee cup in a farewell wave as he strolled out the door. Rose turned back toward the goats. Harry and Sally, huh? What did that tell her about Tate?

Since he'd come to the farm four years ago, Tate had quickly become a regular feature in her life. He came to family dinners. He was invited to her sisters' weddings. He even sat with them at church a good portion of the time.

More than once, Lavender had made comments about how cute he was, or what good friends he and Rose were. But that's all it was. Rose wasn't looking for anything else. In her experience, men made great friends and lousy partners. She'd been "one of the guys" at school and work for as long as she could remember. Growing up with five sisters, hanging out with men was a nice change from life at home. The only problem was that whenever she was interested in someone, they inevitably saw her as a friend. One "helpful" friend in vet tech school had informed her that men didn't want someone who knew the answers or never needed help.

Apparently, to be an attractive woman, you needed to be needy and dumb. And Rose was neither of those things. She couldn't afford to be. Pretending she didn't know what to do last night for baby Harry could have ended in the death of a goat. And for what? To stroke Tate's ego? No way.

Instead, she would do what she needed to do and not worry about the other stuff. Maybe she wasn't meant to get married. Tate was a friend. A friend who made excellent coffee and she liked spending time with. That was all.

TATE's small trailer had been home since he left Montana. It was easier to move around and jump from ranch to ranch when your house had wheels. Of course, it wasn't exactly roomy. But he only slept there anyway.

It had taken his entire first year's salary to buy the camper. Everything he owned fit inside it or the truck. When he told his younger brother he was leaving, Travis hadn't understood. No one had. But Russell Ranch had stopped being home to him when he was seventeen. If it had truly even been home before that.

Since he was old enough to remember, his father had drilled into him that someday the ranch would be his. He saw the pressure his dad was under. He saw how the long hours and unpredictable schedule wore down his mother until she was a shell of a woman. When the ranch did well, his dad was fun and happy. When they struggled? His dad was angry and bitter, taking it out on his wife and kids. For a while, his mom was angry. "What woman wants to be tied to one place her whole life? This ranch will kill both of us if you let it, and you wouldn't even notice." His mother had been crying and yelling at his dad while Tate listened from the dark at the top of the stairs. Soon after that, it was like she'd stopped feeling anything at all. His mom had been right—his Dad either hadn't noticed or hadn't cared.

Tate wanted no part of Russell Ranch or the family he left behind. They had proven over and over again that they only cared about themselves. He would never live like that. Perhaps that was why he had stayed so long with the Bloom Family. Time and time again, he had seen their family put each other ahead of success or pride. When Lily was diagnosed with cancer, the entire family took time off for her appointments or let their own responsibilities slide to help cover events for her.

Tate pulled the pizza from the small oven and set it on the cardboard box to cool. Tonight, there would be no alarm at three o'clock. A full night's sleep would do him well, but he couldn't regret the hours spent in the barn with the animals. And Rose.

She was really something. The whole family was special. Before this job, he hadn't stayed anywhere longer than a year. But there was something about the Bloom family that pulled you in. He remembered his first interview with Laura Bloom. Her kind eyes and genuine smile brought back memories of his own mother—memories from before she'd lost her shine.

They'd chatted casually over coffee in the dining room, the rolling green hills with neat rows of produce painting the perfect landscape out the window. He'd been eighty percent sure he would be turned down for the job based on the interview. She'd asked about his work history and gently probed further when he mentioned his family ranch. A phone call from his father earlier in the week had all his feelings raw and exposed again, and his answer to Laura had been less than kind.

When he got the call from Poppy about the next steps for the job, he'd been shocked. He could still feel Laura's urge to mother him when he joined the family for dinner, but mostly she was kind and supportive and left him alone. Though he knew if he needed anything, the Blooms would step up and help him as though he were family. That was hard to find in a job.

The following weekend, he knocked on Hawthorne's door. Josh, who had married Lily Bloom three years ago, opened the door and waved him in.

"Hey, man, come on in. I thought you might be the pizza."

"Sorry to disappoint," Tate joked. He took off his coat and slipped off his boots. Lily had a reputation as a neat freak, and he was not going to invite her wrath.

He followed Josh back to the living room, where Hawthorne and Emmett were waiting. Emmett was married to another of Hawthorne's sisters, Lavender. He glanced around. "Lance coming tonight?"

Hawthorne shook his head. "No, apparently Daisy is *under the weather*."

Tate looked to Josh for an interpretation of Hawthorne's pointed tone.

Josh shrugged. "We're guessing pregnant, but they haven't announced yet."

Tate smiled. "Nice. Laura will be thrilled, I'm sure."

Hawthorne laughed. "No kidding. She's been subtly hinting that Magnolia and Henry should have cousins by now."

"We've been trying," Emmett admitted quietly from his place on the sofa.

A look of surprise crossed Hawthorne's face. "Whoa, that's huge!" Emmett nodded, but his smile was tight.

"It's been almost a year, but no luck."

"Oh, man. That sucks." Josh laid a hand on Emmett's shoulder. "Can we do anything?"

"It's been really hard on Lavender. We don't know yet if there is anything wrong, but pretty soon we'll start talking to doctors. Apparently, there is something about trying a full year before they'll help you."

"We'll be praying," Josh said firmly.

"Thanks." Their conversation was interrupted by the doorbell and Hawthorne stood up.

"That's the pizza. Help yourself to the drinks in the fridge while I go grab it."

Video games weren't exactly his scene, but Tate enjoyed his time with Hawthorne and the others. It was always a bit unexpected for him when they talked so openly about their faith. When he was growing up, church was something that they did as a family, but only on Sundays. The rest of the week, Jesus wasn't even an afterthought.

Even though he'd been going to church with Rose and her siblings for a year or two, it felt like he was missing something. Rose helped with the high school group during the week, and Lavender was apparently some big author and speaker. Tate believed in God. There was no way he could see the way his crops grew and the way the animals were created without believing that there was a Creator. But other than church on Sunday, he didn't know what he was supposed to do.

There was something different about his friends here though. They talked about Jesus like He was their friend. Like He cared about their lives and helped them through stuff.

Maybe he could ask Rose about it. He shook the thought away as quickly as it came. She wouldn't understand. Her life had been worlds different from his own. Maybe their deep faith was just another way the Bloom family legacy was different from the Russell's.

5

*R*ose woke up early to finish chores and stole downstairs to grab a shower before everyone showed up. Brunch at Bloom's Farm was a family tradition and the one time each week when the family got together.

When she emerged upstairs, the peppery scent of sausage gravy hit her nose. Magnolia and Henry were sitting on Keith's lap as he did an animated reading of Wonky Donkey in his recliner by the fireplace. Rose grinned at their little giggles. She never knew if Poppy and Harrison would be there, but it was always a welcome surprise.

Rose ducked between conversations, heading for the coffee maker. She tapped her brother Hawthorne on the shoulder, then passed him on the other side.

She grinned when he spun in a circle, looking for the culprit.

"Good morning, Mom."

"Good morning, sweetheart. Everything okay with the animals?"

"All good. We even had some eggs today." In the winter, their chickens laid far fewer eggs. There were enough for the immediate family, but no extra. Come summer, they would have enough to sell at farmers' markets or with the CSA baskets Tate managed.

She looked around the kitchen, despite knowing that Tate wouldn't be there. Brunch was for family only and always had been. Tate had come to Sunday dinners or Thanksgiving celebrations over the years, but not to brunch.

It felt like he should be here though. Every week, she looked around for his familiar face and crooked smile, expecting him to raise his coffee cup to her in greeting. Instead, she grabbed her own mug and leaned back against the counter.

Daisy sat on a barstool, her hair in a messy bun. She looked exhausted but smiled up at something Lance said to her. Poppy and Harrison were deep in conversation with Lily and Josh near the table.

"Do you need any help, Mom?"

"Would you set the table for me? Hawthorne," she turned to him, "help your sister set the table."

Avery snickered as Hawthorne objected, protesting that he was talking to Emmett. Avery shoved him toward the fridge. "I'm sure Emmett will survive without that additional knowledge about the Purdue basketball team."

Emmett gave a good-natured chuckle. "Unless you tell me they suddenly created a quidditch team, I'm probably not going to remember anything about what you said." Emmett was a best-selling author of fantasy books, and he and Lavender were far more likely to be caught at a bookstore than a football game.

"No worries, Emmett," Avery assured him. "Hawthorne sometimes forgets that not everyone cares like he does about sportsball. She pointed to herself. "Case in point: his lovely wife."

Rose listened to their exchange while she pulled dishes from the cupboards and carried them to the tables. Lance and his construction crew added the additional dining room off the kitchen last year as a present for Laura from the whole family. As five of the seven children had gotten married, the large kitchen table hadn't been enough room for everyone. Now, the group split across the two rooms.

A few moments later, Laura gently rang the cast iron triangle. "Everyone find a seat. Harrison, would you say grace?"

Rose tried not to roll her eyes. Whenever Poppy and Harrison managed to show up for an event, her mother asked him to say the blessing. Apparently, she thought it might be offensive to have the governor of Indiana over for a meal and not have him say the prayer. Harrison took it in stride and said a quick blessing.

After the chorus of amens, Laura passed biscuits and gravy around the table, along with fresh fruit and sausage links.

Lance stood and cleared his throat. "Excuse me, everyone." The commotion slowly settled and Daisy rose to her feet next to her husband. Rose watched in anticipation. Family brunch was when all the big announcements happened. Engagements, babies, even Lily's cancer three years ago. What could this announcement be?

Hawthorne leaned over to Rose. "Twenty bucks says she's pregnant."

Rose leaned over and nudged him back. "No bet." Daisy was already caressing a hand over her completely flat stomach. Only a fool would take that bet. Plus, knowing Hawthorne, he had insider information.

"We're super excited to share the news that we are expecting! We're due in August."

Cheers erupted around the table, and her mother stood up and rushed over to wrap Daisy in a hug. Rose grinned. Being Aunt Rose to Magnolia and Henry was already super fun. Daisy's son or daughter would be around the farm even more.

Magnolia looked around, trying to figure out what all the excitement was about. Poppy explained, "Aunt Daisy is going to have a baby too. Won't that be fun?"

Magnolia's sweet little voice chimed in. "I'm not a baby. Henry is a baby."

Poppy leaned over with a smile. "That's right. You're my big sweet girl, aren't you?"

Magnolia nodded, but didn't look convinced. Her brother Henry was only eight months old, and Maggie had a hard time adjusting to her parents' attention being split between the two of them.

Hoping to distract her niece, Rose spoke across the table. "Hey, Maggie, I've got something amazing to show you later if you eat all your food!"

"What is it?"

"We've got new baby goats at the barn!" Rose let

the excitement fill her voice and Magnolia responded in kind.

"Oh, baby goats. Can I go, Mommy? Can I?"

"You heard Aunt Rose. Eat your food and we'll go see the animals later."

In response, Magnolia promptly stuffed an entire apple slice in her mouth. Rose pressed her lips together to keep from smiling when Poppy admonished her to take a bite instead. At nearly three, the precocious young girl kept the whole family on their toes.

It would be fun to have another baby around. Hawthorne nudged her with his elbow and she nudged him back. Did he and Avery want to have kids? Avery was pretty focused on her career and her research. Perhaps they were still waiting. Even though she and Avery got along well, Rose had never been comfortable enough to ask. She knew enough to realize it was a sensitive question. It didn't matter to her one way or the other, so Rose merely left the curiosity unsatisfied and figured she would know when they were ready to share anything.

Not every woman wanted to have kids. Andi had made it perfectly clear that it wasn't in her plans. Which brought up another question. Rose got Daisy's attention. "Have you told Andi yet?"

Daisy smiled. "We video chatted with her last night. She said congratulations, and that if I name it Dandelion, she'll disown me." Rose chuckled. Dandelion, more commonly known as Andi, had always hated her name. The only ones who got away with calling her Dandelion were their parents.

"That's so exciting, Daze. Congratulations!"

"Thank you. Right now, I'm mostly tired and wishing my stomach didn't revolt at the thought of a Dr. Pepper."

By late morning, the sun had warmed the day enough to make a walk to the barn a possibility, though everyone was bundled up against the still icy air. Magnolia ran ahead of Rose, Hawthorne, and Poppy. Henry stayed back at the house with Grandma and Grandpa.

Rose picked up Maggie and carried her into the goat pen. The goat kids were jumping around and playing with each other, so Rose pointed them out to her niece. She handed Maggie to Hawthorne and went to pick up Harry. When she brought the small animal over, Hawthorne knelt down so Maggie could pet it. She giggled loudly when Harry's nose nudged her. Poppy snapped photos with her phone.

After the goats, Maggie had to visit the piglets, who had more than doubled in size since she'd last visited. She was upset that the piglets were no longer small and burst into tears. While Poppy tried to explain that animals grow up just like people, Rose saw Tate watching them from the other side of the barn.

"Hey, Tate."

He raised his coffee mug in greeting.

"What brings you down here?" It obviously wasn't unusual to see Tate at her barn. But it was Saturday and he was technically off-duty.

"Just tired of the inside of my trailer. Figured I'd come make myself useful. Maybe take Cappuccino out for a ride."

"Need some company?"

He glanced back at her family. "Sure, if you've got time."

"I've always got time for a ride." That wasn't exactly true. In fact, most of the time she felt bad that the horses didn't get more exercise. They were mostly content in the field, but she loved riding.

"I'll go see if I can get Capp and Mocha to come in from the pasture while you finish up here."

"Sounds good. Thanks, Tate."

6

*T*he horses quickly greeted him when he strolled into the pasture, and he bribed them with sugar cubes to follow him back to their stall. He missed the horses on the ranch back home, and riding the ones at Bloom's Farm was a perk of the job.

When he and Rose were out on the pasture, Tate was wishing he'd worn a winter cap instead of his usual baseball hat. But the sun was shining, and the wind wasn't even whipping across the field like it usually did. He glanced back at Rose. Was she warm enough? Her long, blonde braids disappeared into her stocking cap, and though her cheeks were pink, she looked as happy as he was to be on horseback.

They rode the fence line, checking for broken or sagging barbed wire. The job was easy enough to accomplish from the front seat of a pickup truck or a side-by-side. This was how his father had always done it at home though, and it seemed the Blooms had the same tradition.

"Can I ask you a question, Cowboy?" Rose had started calling him Cowboy when he first arrived on the farm. At first, it had niggled at him. It reminded him of home. But around here, a cowboy wasn't exactly a common sight. When he left Montana, he traded his traditional cowboy hat for a baseball cap, and worked in the oil fields of North Dakota for a season. He'd never gone back, though the hat still rested on top of the refrigerator in his small trailer.

"Depends what it is," he answered honestly.

"Why don't you get a house?"

Tate shrugged a shoulder. "I don't know. What do I need a house for? My trailer serves me fine. And if I—" He cut off midsentence.

"If you what? If you leave?" He could hear the hurt in Rose's voice and it cut like a knife.

"Well, I don't know, Rose. Yeah, I guess. I've never worked anywhere this long. I love it here, but can I really stay forever?" In all honesty, the idea was tempting. Since he'd left home, it felt a little like his soul was searching for that place to dig in and grow roots. Maybe Bloom's Farm was the place.

She was quiet, and he would give anything to know what thoughts were rolling around in her head.

"Is it just a job for you?"

He sighed. "It might have started that way, but I love it here. I love the crazy Midwest weather and all the crops we grow. I love your ridiculous family and your flower names. I even enjoy losing bets to you and being duped into doing the chores you don't want to do. So no, I don't plan on leaving any time soon, Rose." The very thought of leaving sent a wave of pain through his chest. Not seeing Rose every day? He didn't want to examine why the idea bothered him so much. He'd said goodbye to friends before.

"Well, that's good."

"Would you miss me?" he teased.

She swung her leg at him in a half-hearted attempt to kick him from her saddle. "Maybe a little," she admitted.

"You're stuck with me for a while. I just don't see the point in buying a big ole house just for me. You get it, right? I mean, you still live with your parents." He gave a pointed look.

"Yeah, I guess. I've been tossing around the idea

of getting my own place, but I don't want to be too far from the animals. Did you know we each own a piece of the property?"

Tate shook his head. He wasn't exactly surprised. It was a family farm, so he assumed the kids would someday take over the farm. But he didn't realize Rose already owned something.

"Yeah, they gave us each a plot of land a few years back. I've been thinking about getting a trailer like yours."

Tate coughed in surprise as the breath caught in his throat. Rose wanted to live in a dinky travel trailer like his?

"Are you crazy, Rose?"

"What? It'd be nice to have my own place."

"I get that, but you should talk to Lance about building you a little house or something. Have you even seen my trailer? It's not exactly some glamourous tiny house like on those dumb cable shows. It's a camper."

"And?"

"Rose, your bedroom at the main house has more square footage than my entire trailer. You grew up in that big house with the granite counters and the leather couches. You really think you're going to be happy with a pullout sofa bench and a one-burner stove?"

Rose's eyes narrowed. "So, you must have grown up in a pretty rough place to make do with the trailer and all, right?"

Aw, man. She had him there. Growing up on the ranch hadn't been all that different. Big house, comfortable bed. Never went to bed hungry. "It's not the same, Rose."

She pulled Mocha to a stop, and he quickly did the same. "Why? Tell me why the trailer is good enough for you, but not for me."

"Because you're a woman! You should have a couch with too many pillows and a bathroom with a tub for bubble baths." He cut himself off from continuing, because the thought of Rose in a bubble bath was somewhere that his mind did not need to wander.

She blinked at him. "That's the dumbest thing I have ever heard, Tate Russell. For all the years you've known me, have you ever heard me say anything about throw pillows or a bubble bath?"

She had a point. Rose was laid-back, no-nonsense, and hard working. He still didn't think she should park a trailer on the back forty and live out there alone, but apparently, he had stepped knee-deep into a pile of not-his-place. He held up his hands in surrender. "Okay, okay. I just don't think you understand what you'd be getting into, but you're a grown woman. Do what you want." Tate still didn't like the idea of her living out there alone though.

Rose stared at him for a moment, and he resisted the urge to squirm under her gaze. "Thank you," she said curtly before kicking her heels gently to nudge Mocha into motion.

Tate let her get a few yards ahead before he spoke to his horse. "You'd think I'd learn to keep my mouth shut around women, wouldn't you?"

When they made it back to the barn, Rose was obviously still upset with him. He touched her arm as she brushed down Mocha. "Hey, I'm sorry I offended you." When she turned to him, he continued. "If you want to live in a trailer on your little piece of property, who am I to judge?"

"Thanks, I appreciate that."

Then he had an idea. "Tell you what. Before you start shopping for trailers, why don't you borrow mine for a week or two? I can crash with Hawthorne or whatever, and you can see what it's like to live in

200 square feet." Nothing but Rose herself could change her mind about the trailer. But maybe if she actually knew what it was like, she would reevaluate.

Rose pursed her lips as she considered. "You think I should move into your trailer?"

He raised an eyebrow. "It's not like I'm inviting you to stay with me. I'll stay somewhere else." He couldn't help but add something more to make her agree. "I'll bet you a week of packing CSA baskets that you'll admit I'm right by the end of the two weeks."

"And if I'm right and I love it?"

"Then I'll do the hog pen for a month."

"All right, you've got a deal." Tate pumped a fist in the air, and Rose pointed at him with the bristle brush. "You're going to regret this, Cowboy."

She might be right, but he gave her a cheeky grin anyway. She'd be stir-crazy by the third night, he was sure of it.

Rose packed her suitcase with her work clothes, a couple of outfits for church or youth group, and her toiletries. Looking around at the rest of the contents of her room, she considered what else she might need. She'd been in Tate's trailer before, but only a time or two. Did it have a TV? She grabbed her laptop, Bible, and a couple paperbacks, stuffing them into a backpack.

How hard could it be? Tate would be staying at the main house, which her mother had insisted on when she heard about their crazy bet.

"Why on earth are you staying in his trailer?"

"I'm thinking about getting something similar and I want to see how I like it."

Her mother had simply shaken her head and muttered something that sounded remarkably like, "Stubborn like your father," before walking away to prepare a guest room.

It would take some getting used to, she wasn't discounting that. She'd lived with her parents or a roommate her entire life. And it was pretty convenient to know there would be food in the house thanks to her mom and dad.

But she'd shared an apartment during her vet tech program and for the year or two after when she worked in the city. She knew how to cook and didn't mind being alone. This would be a piece of cake, and Tate would be her hog pen cleaner for a whole month. Sign her up for that.

She heard the doorbell ring and her mother greeted Tate like a long-lost relative. Rose carried her things up the stairs. Tate raised an eyebrow and glanced at her bags. "Is that all you've got?"

Rose looked at the single duffel bag he had thrown over one arm. "Is that all *you've* got?" she countered.

Rose's mother shook her head. "What am I going to do with you two? Come on in, Tate. I'll show you your room."

"Thanks again for letting me stay here, Mrs. Bloom."

"Oh, it's my pleasure. I've worried about you out there in that little trailer since you moved in."

"You don't have to worry about me, ma'am. It's just fine for my needs."

Rose watched her mother's eyes slide over to her. "Yes, well. We'll see if Rose thinks it suits her, won't we?"

Rose grinned. "We sure will. It will be fine, Mom."

"Let me drop my stuff and I'll head out there with you," Tate offered. "It's got a few quirks you might want to know about."

Fifteen minutes later, Tate held open the camper door and waved her inside ahead of him. Rose stepped onto the linoleum floor. The strong scent of lemon cleaner met her nose. The entire trailer was remarkably clean. She'd half-expected him to leave it dirty just to reinforce how unsuitable he thought it was for her.

"You cleaned?"

Tate shrugged. "I'm not a cheater. You'd keep your own trailer neat. I couldn't justify sticking you with my mess." He pointed to the right. "Up here is the living room slash dining room." He turned back to the left. "You've got your kitchen here. The bathroom is here, and back there is the bedroom."

Rose followed his verbal tour with her eyes, studying the tight space. There was a bench along one wall, and Tate showed her how the table folded down from the wall.

"Usually I just leave the table down," he explained.

"Here's the stove. The electricity for everything comes from a generator. That includes the heat, the water heater, and the stove. If you cook a lot, you might have to replace the gas tank. So I recommend you keep your showers short."

Rose frowned. She loved long showers, so that was disappointing.

"I didn't pick up any groceries for you, but I

figured you'd want to work that out on your own. The sheets are clean," he said absently.

"Where do you do your laundry?" The question came out sounding far more concerned than she intended it to. She'd never really thought about the fact that Tate wouldn't have his own washer and dryer.

He raised an eyebrow. "I take it to the laundromat in Terre Haute on Sundays after church."

"Oh." That sounded inconvenient. Surely she could simply take them to the main house. "What else do I need to know?"

"The hot water heater will give you about ten minutes of hot water for a shower. Past that, it'll be straight from the well."

She nodded slowly and turned around in the space. She opened the door to the bathroom, her eyebrows shooting skyward when she saw the cramped room and small shower stall. She turned back to Tate. "Do you even fit in that shower?" He wasn't a large guy, but he was taller than her, and his shoulders were strong and broad enough that she had trouble imagining he would fit through the opening.

His cheeks reddened and he shrugged. "I make it work."

She glanced back at the shower. "If you say so.

Enjoy your long, spacious showers at the main house,
I guess."

He grinned. "Oh, I plan to."

7

*S*tanding in the galley kitchen of the trailer with Rose meant they were within arm's reach. If they both turned sideways, there was a buffer of a few inches between them. Her presence seemed to fill the space, and the hint of her minty shampoo wafted toward him each time she turned her head to look at the trailer.

His trailer—where she would sleep for the next two weeks. His bed. His kitchen. He moved toward the bedroom just as Rose stepped toward the dining table. The contact was quick and awkward, and Tate quickly tucked himself against the cabinets to let her pass. He exhaled and shook his head to clear it.

"Um, I've got the TV set up in the bedroom.

There are some DVDs in the cabinet over the head-board if you want to watch something."

Rose smiled. "Okay, thanks. I'll try not to snoop in your things while I'm here."

He shrugged. It wouldn't matter. Living in the camper was a bit like perpetually living from a suit-case. There was no storage for extras. He had some movies and his computer. He kept a few books in the dining room, but mostly he borrowed from the library. "There isn't much else to see."

"Call me if you run into trouble with the heat or anything. The water line is insulated, but if we get a super cold snap, you might have to keep the sink drip-ping to keep it from freezing." He'd double-checked the ten-day forecast and it didn't look like any super cold nights were headed their way. But Rose needed to know the reality of living like he did. It wasn't exactly luxurious. He was lingering now, looking for any last things to say before he was forced to admit it was time to leave Rose out here alone. "You might hear the coyotes at night, but they shouldn't get too close."

He saw a hint of alarm in Rose's eyes and stepped closer. "Are you sure you want to do this?" He kept his voice soft, trying to reassure her it would be okay to back out.

She tipped up her chin. "I'm sure."

He sighed and rubbed a hand over his beard. "Okay. I'm three minutes away if you need me though."

"It's just a camper. I'm fine."

He might have heard a quiver in her voice that betrayed her words, but her eyes were stubborn and her jaw was set. No surprise there. Rose would rather eat dirt than admit she needed someone. He clicked his tongue and nodded. "All right then. I think you're set. I'm going to head to the main house and get settled in. Maybe take a hot shower," he added with a crooked smile.

The comment drew a smile from Rose, and he couldn't resist the urge to pull her into his arms for a hug. It wasn't the first time they'd embraced, and he didn't exactly know why he did it now. He was worried about her though, out here on her own.

Rose tucked her head under his jaw and returned the embrace. "Be safe, Rose."

"I'm fine, Cowboy," she said with a sigh.

He released her and stepped out of the trailer into the cool winter air. With one final look at the trailer, he climbed into his truck and pulled away. Hopefully, he didn't regret this little agreement they made. And he was rather looking forward to a little vacation at the main house.

When he got back, the smell of chocolate and sugar filled the air. Laura must have heard the door, because she came around the corner from the kitchen with a bright smile.

"Everything okay?"

He nodded. "I guess so. I don't know why she is so insistent on proving she can live out there, but she's all set up."

Laura rubbed her hands on a towel. "Rose has a mind of her own. I'm glad she decided to live with us for so long, but I don't blame her for seeking her own space. She'll make the right choice."

The love for her daughter was obvious in Laura's tone, and Tate felt a twinge of envy. His own mother had no idea what kind of man he'd become. Would she be proud? Or would she see his father in him and turn away?

"Come on in and help yourself to a cookie. I forget about you out there in your trailer. You probably haven't had a home-cooked meal since Christmas!"

Tate smiled and pulled off his baseball hat. "You've done an amazing job of making me feel welcome, ma'am. But a cookie sounds perfect." The truth was, over the years, Laura had sent him home with more loaves of banana bread and trays of meat-loaf with potatoes than he deserved.

He wondered again what it would be like to have grown up with a supportive mother and a father who prioritized the family over the farm when necessary. From everything Tate had seen, Keith Bloom would give up everything for his children, including the farm he loved so much. And in return, his children loved the farm enough to stay and help it grow.

Just since Tate had arrived, the bed-and-break-fast that Daisy ran had taken off, the wedding and event venue was booked multiple days each week, and Rose had opened seasonal petting zoo hours. Hawthorne had helped each segment of the farm work together more efficiently.

"What was the farm like when the kids were growing up?"

Laura spoke as she scooped cookie dough onto a baking sheet. "It was a lot different back then. A few animals, mostly for our own benefit. A handful of chickens and a goat. I remember when Keith brought home our first five cows. The kids were so excited." She laughed, "Rose tried to ride one before we even knew what was happening."

Tate laughed. Of course she did. Laura continued. "We had crops, but mostly just corn and soybeans, and the apple orchard. It was a small operation—just Keith and a couple of hired hands. Nothing like the team of employees we have today. I took care of the kids, and of course, they helped too." She smiled, staring into her memories. "It wasn't until the kids were older and took on more responsibility that things really took off. Poppy launched the shift to organic produce, which Keith fought for a while, but eventually embraced. Lily convinced us to take out a loan to build Storybook Barn. And Daisy... She dove headfirst into renovating the old homestead. Before each of our children fought for something they wanted, Bloom's Farm was just like any other farm."

"You must be really proud of them."

"Oh yes, of course. God has been very good to us, and it hasn't always been easy, but I wouldn't trade it for anything."

"That's really nice."

"We're so glad you are here, Tate. I hope you know that."

He stared at the cookie in his hand before smiling politely up at her. "Thanks. I am too."

∾

ROSE SPENT her first night in the trailer tossing and turning on Tate's bed. The sheets were clean, but she swore the pillow still smelled like him. The next morning, Rose got up and stepped into the kitchen, realizing for the first time that Tate didn't have a coffee maker. Where did he make his delicious coffee every morning? His office?

She brushed her teeth in the bathroom, bumping her elbows on the wall and watching herself in the tiny mirror. She considered the shower stall for a moment before deciding that challenge could wait until the evening. Two showers a day was definitely a main house luxury she wouldn't be enjoying in this trailer.

Despite her assurance that she wouldn't snoop, Rose opened every cubby and cupboard she could find in the small trailer. Trailing her finger over the spines of Tate's books, she wondered what was special about those particular titles. The Count of Monte Cristo, A Tale of Two Cities. Plus a tattered hardbound copy of Little Women. That was unexpected.

The DVD selection was equally intriguing. A handful of action flicks and a couple of comedies were mixed among a surprising number of classic romantic comedies. She thought back to the names he'd given the goats and looked at the movies again. There it was. When Harry Met Sally. A smile twitched on her lips and Rose pulled it out. Tate Russell was an enigma of a man, for sure.

Rose had no doubt that if Hawthorne knew about Tate's secret love of romantic movies, their Produce Manager would never hear the end of it.

She tossed the DVD on the bed and planned to watch it later. First, she needed to make a trip to the grocery store. Figuring out what she could cook with one pan and a microwave would be a test. But Rose had never been one to back down from a challenge.

On Monday morning, Rose saw Tate's office light on as she drove from the trailer toward the live-stock barn. Her mouth watered at the thought of coffee she didn't have to make herself, so she parked her Jeep and hurried inside.

"Well, if it isn't Camper Carrie. How was your first weekend flying solo?" Tate scratched his chin. "I didn't see you at church yesterday."

Rose ignored him and poured a cup of coffee. When she turned back around, he was waiting expectantly for a response. She sighed before admitting, "Yeah, my phone got lost between the wall and the bed and I missed my alarm."

A smile played on his lips, but Tate quickly

schooled his features after she glared at him. "Hmm," he replied before lifting his coffee mug.

"And how is living with my parents?" Rose loved her parents, but with no one else living at home, she was sure her mother was desperate for someone to mother.

Tate's features brightened. "Actually, it's pretty awesome. Your mom made chicken parmesan last night and I watched the Purdue game with your dad. I took a shower and didn't end up with a kink in my neck from ducking under the faucet. I might never leave," he said with a grin.

"She's not smothering you?"

Tate's expression was one of confusion. "Not at all. If my mom had been like yours, maybe..."

Rose tipped her head. "Maybe what?"

He jerked a shoulder. "I don't know. Maybe things would have been different. My mom... struggled a lot. Life on a ranch wasn't for her. It made her miserable, and eventually she fell into a cycle of depression too deep to find her way out of. She committed suicide." He stared into his coffee cup.

Her heart broke for the little boy he'd been. "I'm sorry, Tate. I didn't know."

"She wasn't happy. I remember that much. But it still made me wonder what was so terrible about living there with us. I know more about depression now, of course. Which just makes me blame my dad for not caring enough to get her help."

Rose hated that bit of doubt she heard in his voice, so different from the confident, determined man she knew. "It wasn't you. You know that, right?" She needed to reassure him it wasn't his fault.

He looked up at her, and Rose saw the pain in his eyes. "Logically, I know that. I even know that it wasn't entirely my dad's fault, although he certainly didn't help most of the time. It's hard to forgive him for making her life more difficult."

Rose didn't know how to respond to that. Her own father had put his wife above everything, even the children.

Tate continued, "He wasn't an easy man to live with, especially when the ranch wasn't doing well. When I turned eighteen, I knew I didn't want any part of it. It turned him into someone I never wanted to become. So, I left. Dad still probably thinks I'll come back."

Rose's eyes widened. "You don't plan to go back?"

He shook his head. "Nope. It's different here, Rose. Bloom's Farm is as much yours and Hawthorne's as it is your parents. I don't feel like that about Russell Ranch. My memories there aren't all that positive, and I don't want a ranch with that kind of cloud hanging over it. No matter how much Dad wants me to take it."

Rose tried to wrap her mind around the idea of not wanting to run Bloom's Farm. It was in her blood. It was her birthright, even though she was the youngest. She'd been fighting to prove that her entire life. Tate, as the oldest, would probably inherit nearly everything. And he didn't want it?

She wanted to argue with him, to shake him by the shoulders and tell him to realize what a blessing it was that his father wanted to hand over the reins to him from the beginning. But she also saw the vulnerability in Tate's expression and the stubborn way he declared his disinterest. She wouldn't change his mind.

But it reinforced something she already knew deep in her heart. She and Tate could be great friends and colleagues. But they wanted very different things in life. Whatever random thoughts she'd had about the possibility of more between them were better off ignored.

"Thanks for telling me about your mom. You're welcome to enjoy mine any time. She's always happy to mother someone."

Tate's lips slowly drew into a smile. "Thanks."

Rose lifted her coffee cup in a silent acknowledgement before taking another swallow. "I better head down and start my day. It's inoculation day for the goats."

Tate lifted a hand and turned back to his computer as she made her way to the door. Their conversation had turned pretty serious this morning. She'd have to make fun of him for his taste in movies another time.

Keith Bloom was sitting at the kitchen table, a notebook and a Bible spread out in front of him.

"Good morning, Mr. Bloom."

"You can call me Keith, you know."

Tate smiled. "Yes, sir. What are you doing up so early this morning?" Usually Tate didn't see the Bloom patriarch until later in the day, and Tate was up early to check on the cucumbers they had transplanted outside last week.

"Couldn't sleep. I figured I'd come out here and see what God was trying to tell me."

Tate gave a puzzled frown. "You think God's trying to tell you something?"

Keith smiled kindly. "He usually is, if I take the time to listen. Do you take time to listen to God, Tate?"

Tate scooped grounds into the coffee maker and shook his head. "I don't really know. I'm not sure He'd have much to say to me anyway." After he filled the machine with water, Tate sat down at the table and waited for the coffee to brew.

"It's easy to think God is too busy to be concerned with our lives. After all, what is one little farm in the grand scheme of the world?" Keith looked out the window, and Tate followed his gaze to the sunrise peeking over the hill. "But there is a verse that says God cares about the smallest things, like a simple sparrow. It says we are far more important than a sparrow." Keith turned back to him, and Tate saw wisdom and genuine compassion in his eyes. "Tate, God wants to hear from you. And He wants to speak into your life. He wants a relationship."

Tate tried to process everything Keith was saying. "How?" The question seemed simple, but it felt monumental to him. God had always been something he learned about on Sundays. God created the world. Jesus died for him. But this idea that God really cared about his life? It was foreign and a little intimidating.

Keith explained how his daily prayers and reading the Bible helped him connect to God. And as Tate listened to his words, it made sense.

"You've given me a lot to think about, Keith." Tate stood up and filled his coffee cup, trying to find the words he was looking for. "Would you... Would you mind if I ask you more questions if I have them?"

Keith's smile grew and he leaned back in his chair. "I'd like that very much. Any time at all."

The friends he had here, Emmett and Josh and the entire Bloom family—they spent time with God. Not just church on Sundays, but actually talking to God and reading the Bible. He'd always been able to see it in their lives and the way they spoke about their faith. But now he had an explanation.

And now he really wanted to do it too.

8

*F*our days into her trailer adventure, Rose was seriously regretting the decision. After Tank had knocked her into the mud earlier today, there was nothing she wanted more than to sit under a steaming shower and ease her sore muscles. She'd even considered going to the main house, but the thought of seeing Tate's smug expression forced her back to the miniscule shower stall at the trailer instead.

When the water grew cold, she stepped out and threw on her pajamas. Her phone chimed with a text message.

TR: Storms rolling in. You good?

Rose tapped the weather app and saw the line of storms he was talking about. There was a storm watch and a pretty good deal of red and orange marching across the radar map. Not ideal, but not unusual for the early Indiana spring.

RB: All good. Thunderstorms are my favorite.

She grabbed a sandwich for a quick dinner and settled onto the bed with her laptop. An hour later, she heard the rain on the roof of the trailer. The rhythm of the rain slowly lulled her to sleep as the movie continued playing on her computer.

A booming crash of thunder startled her awake, and she looked around, slightly disoriented. Wind howled around the exterior of the trailer. Her phone chimed and she saw the weather alert for a severe thunderstorm. Her pulse kicked up a notch, but Rose grew up in Indiana. She was no stranger to storms. There were a few more unread text messages and a missed call from Tate.

TR: The storm looks bad. Maybe you should come to the house.

TR: Don't ignore me! I'm tempted to come get you myself.

Rolling her eyes at his paranoia, Rose opened the local news channel website and pulled up the livestream coverage of the storm as thunder crashed outside. Tate wasn't from around here. This would blow over just like every other storm she'd experienced while living in the Midwest.

The website loaded, and the meteorologist's voice filled the small bedroom.

"We have reports that minutes ago, a tornado crossed highway 41, approximately 4 miles north of the 41/63 interchange. It is traveling north northeast at 25 miles per hour. If you are in the path of the storm, please take shelter immediately." The map on the screen showed Rogers county in red, and the meteorologist drew an arrow to represent the tornado. Rose gasped and sat up, tucking her legs under her. She crawled to the edge of the bed and peeked through the blinds on the small windows. Lightning flashed, and she saw nothing but dark skies and empty pasture. The trees in the distance were bending under the force of the wind.

Okay, maybe this time there was actually a reason to be concerned. She knew exactly where the intersection was, and it wasn't far from the farm.

Rose looked around the small camper. Where should she go? Should she try to drive to the main house? She stood up and walked the four steps to the kitchen. Then looked back at the bed, her mind racing. She grabbed her keys and headed for the door.

The phone in her hand chimed again and a notification flashed. She saw the words "TORNADO WARNING" at the top of the message. Why hadn't she been paying attention? How could she have fallen asleep?

It was then that she realized the normally quiet camper suddenly filled with unbearable noise. It sounded like she was standing next to the tracks as a train rushed by. She froze in place, but the trailer rocked and shifted in the wind. Her feet were unsteady beneath her as the floor rocked like a boat on the waves, threatening to toss her into the cabinets along the wall.

Not sure what else to do, Rose stumbled into the small hallway that connected the kitchen to the bedroom and sank to the floor. She pulled her knees to her chest and hung her head between them, clapping her hands over her ears.

She yelled desperate prayers inside her head, as the noise around her grew louder still. Rose squeezed her eyes shut. Ragged breaths escaped painfully and her heart hammered in her chest. There was a crash to her left, the floor shuddered beneath her.

Distantly, Rose heard someone scream. Then she realized the screaming was coming from her.

TATE HAD TRIED CALLING Rose again a few minutes ago, but there was no signal. His heart sank and a feeling of dread washed over him. He should have driven out there to get Rose when he'd thought about it. She'd probably resent him for thinking she couldn't handle it herself, but that shouldn't have stopped him.

Like he had been with nearly every severe storm since he'd moved here, Tate had been glued to the TV and unable to relax. Keith Bloom, on the other hand, appeared to have been woken from a dead sleep as he hurried down the stairs with Laura.

"It's just a storm. It's going to be okay," Keith's words did little to reassure him as they both stared out the walkout basement door.

"No, it's not! Rose is out there, and the weatherman said it's headed right towards us." Tate heard the anguish in his own voice. "She wouldn't answer my texts. I should go get her, right? She must be asleep."

Lightning flashed and highlighted the silhouette of a tornado against the sky. It looked to be about a quarter mile south of the main house.

Keith gasped. Immediately, Tate turned to run

up the stairs and into the rain outside, stumbling down the stairs and thankful for his keyless entry and push start. He threw his truck in park and drove as quickly as he dared toward his trailer—and his friend. His stomach churned. The drive seemed to take twice as long as he remembered.

As he got close, he could see the path of the tornado in the uprooted earth and trees. He swerved to avoid broken fences and tangled barbed wire that had been tossed across the road. If Rose was hurt, this was all his fault. He clenched his jaw, his gaze darting across the destroyed landscape.

When he crested the hill and saw the small lot where he'd parked his trailer, a strangled cry escaped from his throat.

Rose's jeep was lying upside down, having been tossed into the trailer like a Hot Wheels car in the hands of baby Henry. It rested inside the giant hole it had ripped in the front side of the trailer.

Where was she?

Rain stung as it sliced against his skin, his t-shirt already soaked and clinging to his chest. He yelled her name, praying for a response.

The door of the trailer was partially caved in and he wrenched it open and off the hinges. "Rose!"

"Tate?" At the sound of her voice, the vise grip around his heart released.

He ducked into the wrecked trailer and tried to orient himself in the debris.

"Over here!" He turned to the left and saw a flash of light. She held up her cell phone flash light, and he saw her huddled frame between the wall and the closet door.

"Rose, thank God. Are you okay?" He knelt next to her and tried to examine her for injuries. She was vibrating and shaking her head repeatedly.

"It's okay, sweetheart. You're okay. Look at me, I'm here." When her eyes met his, the absolute fear in them twisted his gut. "It's okay. The tornado is gone. You're safe."

She ducked her head, and he pulled her into his arms. She shuddered as a sob finally broke through her.

He stroked her hair and let her cry. "Are you hurt? Say something, please. I just have to know if you're all right."

He felt another release of tension when she shook her head. "No, I'm okay. I just..."

"Shhh, it's fine. You don't have to talk about it." He looked back toward the Jeep sitting only feet away, where his dining room table used to be. It could have been so much worse. "Come on, let's get you home." He helped her to her feet, though his own were unsteady beneath him. He blew out a deep breath and rubbed his hands over his face. Rose was okay. Nothing else mattered right now.

Rose tripped as she followed him out of the camper, and Tate swept her into his arms. The rain continued to pound on top of them and he hurried to the passenger side of the truck. He started to lift her into the seat, but she pushed away from him and shook her head.

"I'm okay," she insisted as she climbed inside. Tate felt a twinge of hurt at her stubbornness, but brushed it away. It was a good sign that she didn't want his help, right?

He drove her to the main house, stealing a glance in her direction every few moments. During the ride, Rose seemed to withdraw into the seat. She held her knees close and had her feet up on the seat, huddled into a tight ball as though to hold herself together.

When he pulled into the driveway, Laura and Keith were waiting at the front door and quickly opened it as they walked inside.

"She's okay," he quickly reassured them when Rose didn't speak. "The trailer got hit, but she's okay. It was so close though."

Laura led them to the living room, where a fire roared. He watched as Rose sat gently on the couch, joined immediately by her mother. Rose curled into Laura and wept.

"I was so scared, Mom. I thought I was going to die." Her words escaped in a torrent of tears, and Tate's heart broke at the obvious fear and trauma in her voice.

Tate stood by, feeling helpless as Laura comforted her daughter. Why had he even offered Rose to stay in his trailer? This was all his fault. It should have been him out there tonight.

"I'm so sorry, Rose. I should never have let you stay there." He paced in front of the fire, hurling mental admonishments at himself.

A heavy hand on his shoulder stopped his constant motion and the string of self-directed, angry words. He met the calm, weathered eyes of Keith Bloom.

"It's not your fault, son."

Tate shook his head in denial. "If I hadn't—"

"If you hadn't torn out of here like a bull from the chute, Rose might still be out there instead of back here safe with us." Keith squeezed his shoulder and held his gaze, waiting.

Eventually, Tate nodded. "Yes, sir."

9

*R*ose laid in bed, unable to sleep. Each time she closed her eyes, she felt the bed shift below her like the floor had when the Jeep struck the camper. The memory of the deafening roar of the wind overwhelmed her, despite the mostly quiet night.

A crack of thunder had her bolting upright and gasping for breath.

The first rays of light snuck around the curtains, and Rose let out a sigh of relief. Attempting to sleep was exhausting. She might as well get up and try to do something useful.

Trying to process what had happened last night seemed an impossible task. Was it all just a bad dream? Or was she really rescued from the wreckage of Tate's trailer?

Here she was in her own bedroom, so apparently the answer was yes.

She got up and went upstairs, moving on autopilot to the coffee pot.

"Morning."

At the voice behind her, Rose jolted and her hand flew to her heart. She turned to see Tate sitting at the table, his own mug steaming in front of him.

"Oh! I didn't even notice you there."

"Sorry, I didn't mean to scare you."

She turned back to get a mug and pour her coffee, reprimanding her racing heart. "It's fine. Just caught me off guard."

"How're you doing this morning?" Tate's tone was cautious, like he was treading lightly near a wounded animal.

She turned and leaned back against the counter, wrapping her hands around the warmth of the ceramic in her hands. Rose exhaled, disguising her sigh as an attempt to cool her coffee. "I'm okay, I guess. I still don't know that I have fully processed what happened, you know. Like, one minute I'm on the bed watching a show on my computer and the next minute I'm huddled in the hallway praying for my life. And then it was like the world caved in." She froze. "Oh my word, Tate. Your trailer! I didn't even look last night, is it even livable?"

A sad smile crossed his features and he shook his head. "Uh, no. You were honestly lucky it wasn't worse. The whole front half of the trailer is destroyed. Your Jeep didn't exactly escape unscathed either."

Rose tried to remember last night, but in the storm's aftermath, she only remembered Tate's voice and the warmth inside his truck. And in his arms.

She moved to the table and sat in the chair next to his. "Well, that sucks."

He clicked his tongue. "I guess." He paused. "Honestly, I can't manage to be anything but grateful that you're okay. When I drove up and saw the trailer, I wasn't sure what I would find inside." His voice was raw and strained, and she saw the anguish on his face.

Rose laid her hand across the table and rested it on his forearm. "Thanks for coming." His eyes were on her hand and she squeezed lightly before removing it.

His voice was quiet when he replied. "I couldn't *not* come, Rose."

Rose met his gaze and tried to translate the

emotion she saw in the rich, dark depths. They were best friends, but was that all he meant? She didn't know how to respond.

Tate cleared his throat. "I'm sure you want to check the animals after that storm, but sometime today we should go take pictures and salvage what we can from the trailer. I've got to check the greenhouse and the barn too."

Rose nodded. The animals would be a little wound up after a storm like that, and she needed to make sure none of the fences had been damaged. The last thing she wanted was to go wrangle a stubborn cow off the highway and back into the pasture.

They made a plan for the day and finished their coffee. When they stood, Tate grabbed her mug and set it back on the table. Then he wrapped his arms around her. She let herself melt into his embrace, because the sheer act of holding it together for the past thirty minutes had been about the limit of her capability this morning.

She stood there in his arms for what could have been minutes. A few tears escaped onto his flannel work shirt, but they exchanged no words.

When they finally broke apart, Tate held her shoulders and met her gaze. "I'm glad you are safe. But you don't have to be okay if you aren't. Got it?"

She nodded and mustered a grateful smile. How could he know those were exactly the words she needed to hear? She wasn't okay. Not by a long shot.

TATE FISHED soggy books from a puddle near the trailer. None were too special, except the old copy of Little Women that had belonged to his mother. He briefly considered if it was worth trying to salvage, but as he held it up, water dripped from the spine. It was a lost cause.

Anger flashed through him. He had so few possessions, why did it have to be his home that was destroyed? He dropped the book back in the mud and continued to survey the area. Broken dishes and pieces of siding sprinkled the nearby field.

Tate snapped photos with his phone since they'd need them for insurance. He tried to survey the scene like someone whose entire life wasn't spilled across the ground. The trailer door rested on the grass near the opening, where he vaguely remembered tossing it as he searched for any sign of Rose.

He ducked inside the caved-in entrance and walked toward the bedroom. The floor in the kitchen was slippery with pooled rainwater. The further he got away from the dining area, the more normal things appeared. In the bedroom, the blankets were only slightly rumpled. Rose's laptop still sat on the bed, though it was upside down.

His eyes descended to the floor in the doorway where Rose had sought meager shelter from the storm. Tate still couldn't bear to think about how close she'd been to serious injury—or worse. If the tornado had been stronger, it could have lifted the entire trailer and tossed it a hundred yards across the pasture.

As he stared back toward the exposed undercarriage of the Jeep, Rose poked her head inside the door. "Hey, Cowboy."

He smiled. "Be careful, it's wet. I was going to gather some of your stuff, but you could stay outside."

Rose shook her head and walked toward him. "It's okay."

He stood in the bedroom, in the small walkway between the wall and the foot of the bed. He watched her face carefully as she stepped into the doorway. She seemed almost determined to ignore the significance of the spot. Following her lead, Tate pressed on with the task at hand. He closed the laptop and handed it to her. Working together, they pulled her clothes from the small closet and loaded them into his truck.

He was grateful for the help, but he knew Rose couldn't afford to spend all day cleaning up the mess. "Don't you have things to do at the barn?" He had been glad to discover the greenhouses untouched by the storm. The tornado had cut a path through one field, mostly tomatoes and carrots, but the path was narrow and the rest of the plants would be fine. There wasn't anything he could do about it. But Rose would have fences down and troughs to flip and refill.

Rose gathered an armful of DVDs and a few miscellaneous items he'd stored in the bedroom. "Tate, you are family, and your home was just destroyed. Hawthorne's taking care of things, and then he'll be up here too."

Tate felt a wave of gratitude for his friends. He met Rose's gaze, "Thanks." She simply nodded and they got back to work. The food in the refrigerator was spoiled, but they loaded anything from the kitchen and bathroom cabinets into boxes Rose had brought with her.

For now, they decided to leave most of the debris. He had insurance. Surely, it wouldn't take too long to get the initial assessment completed. Until then,

Tate would stay at the main house. The two-week vacation of luxury had suddenly become a lot less entertaining.

He would miss his camper. It was one of the few large purchases he'd made as an adult, earned with his own money from the oil fields of North Dakota. It wasn't a house, like his friends from high school were buying to raise their kids in. But it was his. Or at least, it had been until last night.

Now that some of the shock was wearing off, the rest of the impact of the storm was sinking in. He couldn't live with Keith and Laura forever. For several reasons, but mostly his pride wouldn't let him. Would it be wise to see Rose even more than he already did? This morning, they'd shared their coffee over the kitchen table and chatted as the sun came up. It felt enticingly domestic, and Tate didn't want to let himself go there. He and Rose were just friends.

He wouldn't be tied to one place, especially with a wife in the picture. Logically, he knew Rose wasn't his mother. He bit back a smile. His own mother wouldn't have been caught with her hand inside a pregnant goat if the Hope Diamond was hidden inside. Rose would never leave Bloom's Farm. And he couldn't stay. What if the tornado wrecking his camper was God's way of telling him it was time to move on?

Tate let out a heavy sigh. These thoughts were far too deep and energy consuming after the longest night of his life. For now, he could go back to the main house, grab a hot shower that lasted far too long, and pretend he wasn't reevaluating his entire current life situation.

10

A few days later, Rose sought out Tate at the greenhouse. She found him surrounded by parts and tools as he scoured an equipment manual.

"Hey, Cowboy. Is it a bad time?"

Tate looked up and groaned. "It's the perfect time. I've been fighting with this humidifier for an hour, and I'm about to take it out to the pasture to use for target practice."

Rose raised her eyebrows. "If you get that far, I'll grab my rifle and take a couple shots. I haven't been shooting since last summer." Rose had received her first BB gun when she was six, and was a better shot than all of her siblings, not including Andi, but most definitely including Hawthorne.

Tate stood up and stretched. Rose's eyes hung on

the way his shirt stretched across his chest and shoulders as he arched his back. "What brings you to my neck of the farm?"

"I need to vent to someone and Tank just doesn't make a great listener."

Tate smiled and nodded. "Okay, I'm all ears."

Rose started pacing. "Everyone is treating me like some fragile, broken little bird after the tornado thing."

She saw Tate's eyebrow raise. "Tornado *thing?*" he echoed.

"Yes! I get it. I could have died. But it's getting ridiculous. Hawthorne wouldn't even say Twister's name the other day." Twister was the name of one of the male goats. "Like he thinks I am going to fall into hysterics at the mere mention of what happened." She waved her arms and let her frustration show. "I'm not some breakable piece of glass that can't handle adult conversations."

Tate leaned against a shelving unit—a still, solid contrast to her agitated state of constant motion.

"Is this one of those things where you only want me to listen and say mm-hmm and don't want me to give actual advice?" Rose pursed her lips. It was a reasonable question, but she didn't know for sure what she was looking for. He shrugged. "I'll do whatever you want, but I need to know what I'm stepping into here."

Rose felt the pull of a smile tug at her cheek. She rolled her eyes. "Fine. Advice, I guess." He opened his mouth, but she interrupted him. "It's just so frustrating. My mom tried to make me chamomile tea last night." She gave an exaggerated gagging face. "Okay, I'm done. Now advice."

Tate paused. "You sure?" She nodded, and Tate closed the distance between them. "You almost died. People were scared. You can feel however you want to about the situation. If you are fine, great. If you are having nightmares or whatever, that's fine too." He laid his hands on her shoulders. "But everyone else gets to feel the way they do, too. If your mom wants to make you chamomile tea to remind herself that she didn't lose her baby girl, then let her. If Hawthorne wants to walk on eggshells out of concern for you, then so be it." He was even closer now, and she had to tip her head up to maintain eye contact.

"If I wanted to kiss you, because the thought that something almost took you away forever is driving me crazy and I need to reassure myself that you are here..." Rose's mouth fell open in shock. What did he say? Before she could process it, he turned away. "All

I'm saying, Rose, is that everyone is going to react to this differently. Cut them some slack."

She froze in place, blinking as her brain tried to catch up with him. Was he saying he wanted to kiss her? Or was he being hypothetical? She cleared her throat. "Um, okay. That makes sense. I should try to be less annoyed at people?"

Tate nodded. "Yep. They don't think you are weak or fragile, Rose. Everyone who knows you knows that isn't true. But they did come face to face with the possibility that they might lose you." His voice dropped, and he seemed almost to be talking to himself. "That could make anyone act out of character and do something they'd normally never do." With his words, he was crossing the space between them again in two quick strides.

One strong arm wrapped around her waist and pulled her closer. Instinctively, Rose tipped her head up to meet him, and her eyes drifted closed. She waited. The warmth of his skin was close to hers, but he stopped. Her eyes fluttered open, and she saw the pain and desire in the dark brown pools of his eyes.

"I almost lost you, Rose," he whispered.

"I'm right here." She closed her eyes again and lifted onto the balls of her feet.

Finally, when she thought perhaps he'd changed

his mind, his lips met hers. Rose sank into the kiss, memorizing every sensation. She tucked her hands around to the small of his back and drank in the ecstasy of being thoroughly kissed.

EVERY NERVE ENDING EXPLODED the moment Tate's lips landed against the impossibly soft curve of Rose's mouth. She was right here, a freaking miracle in his arms, and he never wanted to let go. Her hands wrapped around his waist, and he pulled her closer still. He loved everything about the way she felt against him. The way she tasted and the small hums of satisfaction he could hear in her throat.

He slid one hand up her arm and teased the hairs that always escaped the braids at the nape of her neck. Four years in the making, he wouldn't waste a second of this kiss regretting or overthinking it. He would simply pour all of his fear and gratitude and surrender into it and hope she could translate.

Tate broke the kiss and pulled away slightly. His arm was still around her middle and his palm cradled her jawline. The pale skin was soft and warm against his hand, and she pressed into the contact.

"I probably shouldn't have done that," he said quietly.

Rose's eyes flew open. "What is that supposed to mean?"

Tate smiled at her feisty reaction. "I've just been struggling with this idea that I almost lost you. It isn't fair for me to assume you have the same feelings for me." He felt her try to pull away, and he released the hand on her waist.

Rose stepped back and crossed her arms. "You know what they say about when you assume." She raised her eyebrow in a challenge.

Tate ran a hand over his beard. "Yep," he said with a sigh as he dropped his eyes to his boots. "I'm sorry. It was just this crazy reaction. It won't happen again."

"You're a dummy," Rose said.

In a flash, his eyes were on her face. He narrowed his eyes. "What now?"

"You heard me. You kissed me. But did I seem like an unwilling participant?" Tate felt the heat rise in his cheeks at her words. She'd definitely participated. "I'm going to go. If you decide you want to kiss me again, and not because of some weird, morbid realization—then let me know. Otherwise, I'll see you around."

With that proclamation, Rose was out the door and marching back down the hill. The door slammed behind her. Tate winced at the noise and then exhaled. Really messed that one up, hadn't he? He watched her through the greenhouse windows until she disappeared out of sight.

The greenhouse was silent, save for the quiet buzzing of the grow lights and the constant drone of the heater. His eyes landed back on the pile of tools and parts from his earlier project. With one last glance toward Rose's retreat path, he sat back down to tackle his job. The memory of that kiss would probably have him struggling to read the manual, but it had been one heck of a kiss.

11

*R*ose tossed a coil of barbed wire, her Kevlar and leather gloves, the shovel, and her tin snips in the bed of the Ranger and shoved the key into the ignition.

He shouldn't have done that. What did he even mean, he shouldn't have done that? That kiss had been the most fantastic, out of this world kiss of her entire thirty-year existence. And he shouldn't have done it? Coward.

The worst part was that most of her body was yelling at her to turn around and march back into the greenhouse. From there, it was a tossup whether she would give him a piece of her mind, or simply show him how much of not-a-mistake it was for them to kiss again.

Instead, she punched the gas pedal and tore off into the pasture. Hawthorne had repaired the fences where the herds were currently pastured, but the other sections of the property had likely seen strong enough winds to do some damage.

She followed the fence line, walking where it disappeared into patches of trees and her vehicle couldn't reach. When she found a downed branch that had knocked a post loose and turned the barbed wire fence into a saggy, ineffective barrier, Rose trudged back to the Ranger and grabbed the chainsaw and her safety glasses.

After cutting and removing the large limb, she restrung the wire and filled in the hole around the fence post. She gave it a solid shake. It'd hold well enough. All the while, she was debating what to do about Tate.

Her entire thought process about him had changed in an instant. She knew him. Rose probably knew Tate better than she knew Hawthorne. But in her mind, he'd always been firmly in the friend category, despite his rugged good looks and incredibly generous nature.

When he first showed up on the farm, she'd thought maybe there was potential there. But she'd quickly followed his lead and never tried for anything more. Maybe she should have tried to flirt.

She scoffed at her own foolishness. Flirting was not a skill that Rose had worked on over the years. No wonder the man had never hit on her. For crying out loud, he'd seen her up to her elbow in a mama goat! Nothing sexy about that.

The light was fading and with a sigh, Rose turned the Ranger around and headed back to the barn. They'd be fixing these fences for weeks. The tornado winds had done some major damage.

When Rose got back to the main house, she slipped off her boots and waved to her parents, who were each reading in the living room. Such a peaceful scene.

She was sorry Tate lost his trailer, but she didn't miss the camper shower. After a nice long soak, she emerged from the basement bathroom in her robe, absently toweling her long, blonde hair. Rose jumped at the sight of someone sitting on the sectional in the basement living room.

"Nice robe," Tate's voice was teasing and a little sarcastic. Rose glanced down at the terry cloth robe, which was red and covered with pink and white hearts. It had been a Valentine's gift from her mom nearly a decade ago and was admittedly starting to show its age.

She ignored him and disappeared into her room. She shut the door and turned around aimlessly. Why was he down here? Did he want to talk? Did he want to kiss? What was she doing right now?

Take a deep breath. It's no big deal. It's just Tate. She felt herself starting to feel rushed, knowing that he was waiting just outside. She forced herself to slow down. Taking her sweet time, Rose got dressed and brushed her hair. He could wait a little longer.

After twenty minutes had passed, there was a light knock on the door. "Are you coming back out?"

She marched over to her bedroom door and flung the door open. Tate had his forearm resting on the doorframe, and his white undershirt lifted slightly from the waist of his jeans. She swallowed to moisten her suddenly desert-dry mouth. "What do you want?"

He glanced inside. "Purple, huh?"

Rose glared at him, but ignored his comment about the color of her walls. She raised an eyebrow. He sighed and shifted his weight. "Can we talk?"

She stepped under his arm and out into the living area. It seemed safer than her bedroom.

"I'm sorry."

"For..." she continued for him.

"You really aren't going to make this easy, are you?" He pulled his cap off and ran a hand through his hair before jamming the hat back down.

She bit back a smile and shook her head. "Nope."

His dark eyes met hers. "I'm sorry I didn't let you know just how much I enjoyed that kiss."

Now they were getting somewhere. Then he continued, "I really shouldn't have kissed you without asking, but you did kiss me back. Which was the entire point you made earlier."

So close, Tate. He was hopeless. She pressed her lips together in irritation before responding, "Okay."

"That's it? Okay?"

"Mm-hmm. Is that everything?" She lifted her eyebrows and waited expectantly.

"Wait, what?" His confused look was surprisingly adorable.

The man was clueless. "Thanks for stopping by. I'm going to go grab dinner upstairs."

"I'm confused."

Obviously. "You say that as though it is unusual for you."

"It is unusual. And unexpected."

"Tell me something, Cowboy. What did you expect to happen when you apologized?"

"I don't know, Rose!" She could tell Tate was frustrated now, which was exactly what she wanted. She'd been feeling that way all day.

"Then I guess we're done here."

"What if I don't want to be done?"

Could he give her any more mixed signals? Rose stepped close to him and placed her hands on the waistband of his jeans, his bare skin teasing the tips of her fingers. His woodsy scent tickled her nose. She lowered her voice to a whisper and tried to push him to the edge. "Is this what you want, Cowboy?"

ROSE WAS IMPOSSIBLY CLOSE, the aroma of her soap and shampoo clouded his senses. Tate gave a groan and stepped out of her reach. "I don't know! We're friends, right? We work together. We help each other around the farm and bet on the worst chores. I'm not supposed to kiss you!"

"Why not? What is it exactly that makes me so unkissable?" She grabbed her still-wet hair and shook it. "Is it my hair? Is it my less-than-ladylike knowledge about the sperm count of Tank? What? What is it about me that means I'm good friend material, but not good enough to kiss?"

Tate had never seen Rose this fired up, and that was saying something. Fire he could handle. The problem was the absolute nonsense that was coming out of her mouth. It wasn't that she wasn't good enough. Quite the opposite, actually.

Rose Bloom was the owner's daughter. The boss's sister. His best friend. She was far, far too good for him. And the last thing he should do is entertain crazy fantasies about turning their friendship into something more.

"Don't be crazy, Rose. It's not about you! It's about us. We wouldn't work. It was a kiss that shouldn't have happened."

"It was a kiss that should go down in the hall of fame of kisses," Rose retorted.

Tate stuffed down the caveman-esque sense of satisfaction at the comment. He couldn't disagree with her evaluation of the kiss though. It had been spectacular, but it couldn't have a repeat performance. With that in mind, he pushed forward with what he'd been saying. "I let my emotions get the best of me, and I won't let it happen again." He spoke firmly, as though he could sway both of them if he was convincing enough.

"Well, that's entirely disappointing." Rose

turned on her heel and went up the stairs to the main floor.

Tate blew out a breath and scraped a hand over his face and beard after the sound of her footsteps had faded. "Yeah. It really is," he voiced his agreement to the empty room.

ate escaped into a whirlwind of activity as the spring planting and transplanting season consumed his time and energy. Despite still living in the main house with Rose and her parents, he saw surprisingly little of her. Which was probably for the best. He still found his thoughts lingering on the kiss and the confrontation in the basement more often than was healthy.

At least his conversations with Keith Bloom were a good distraction. Keith was turning out to be a fount of wisdom and encouragement. At his encouragement, Tate had downloaded a Bible app on his phone and started reading Ephesians.

It was a new experience for him. Despite years in

church, he couldn't remember ever reading the Bible on his own. He ended up with more questions than answers, but Keith reassured him that was normal. Slowly Tate grew more comfortable with the passages and talking to God. He still wasn't convinced there was something God was trying to tell him like Keith insisted, but he found he enjoyed the time spent in the Word. His days seemed a little less frantic, and he felt more at peace about the destruction of his camper.

The thoughts of Rose though? They still had him tied up in knots. When he got a text from her and read the message, he immediately grinned.

RB: I bought a clay pigeon thrower from someone at church. I hereby wager that I can beat you in a skeet shooting competition.

TR: Stakes?

Rose responded quickly. She must have already known what she wanted.

RB: If I lose, I'll do two Saturday farmers' markets of your choice. If I win, you have to install my new water tank for the pigs.

Tate considered his odds. He was decent with a shotgun, but it had been years since he'd shot for fun or gone hunting. He would love to have a free Saturday or two this spring. Plus, if he won, he could usually convince Rose to go double-or-nothing and he'd end up even further ahead.

TR: I hereby accept the terms of your wager.

He received a smiley face back from Rose. Back to friends like they were meant to be.

TR: Supposed to be nice Saturday, plan on after brunch?

SINCE TATE WAS LIVING in the house, he was officially invited to brunch on Saturdays, which made Rose's life very uncomfortable. Emmett had mistakenly assumed they were dating the first time Tate came. Despite Lavender quickly shushing her husband, the awkwardness had already settled over the table.

Rose felt like she was constantly defending their relationship as just friends to her nosy sisters, while bemoaning the same privately. She hadn't spent much time with him, but she was painfully aware that Tate was just upstairs every night. Instead of taking her coffee from the kitchen, she'd started leaving through the walk-out basement and only drinking coffee in the barn.

But enough was enough. She missed her friend.

And the clay pigeon thrower had popped up in a discussion with one of the other youth group volunteers. Before she knew it, Rose was the proud owner of a foot-activated thrower.

She'd been debating how to reestablish a friend connection with Tate, and a wager was the perfect thing. It had been a few years, but her shooting skills were solid. She really didn't want to install the new water tank, so even the chance to make Tate do it instead was a win in her book.

Saturday afternoon, the thrower was set up over an empty pasture. Most of her siblings and their spouses stuck around to watch. Lance even brought Daisy a lawn chair to sit in while she watched the competition.

"Go, Rose! You got it." The encouragement did little to calm her nerves. She grabbed a box of shotgun shells and put it in her vest compartment.

"Hey, Annie Oakley. Ready to lose?" Tate's taunting was entirely expected, but Rose rolled her eyes.

"I'm ready to watch you lose, does that count?"

Her brother-in-law, Josh, stepped between them and role-played an over-the-top game show host. "The game coin is this perfectly ordinary quarter. Ladies first. You may call the toss," he said to Rose.

"Rose Bloom, you have won the toss! Would you like to shoot first or defer?" Rose heard her sisters cheer when Josh announced her pre-victory win.

"I'll defer, thank you." Rose always performed best under pressure, so having Tate shoot before her would help her shoot on target.

Tate flashed her a grin and loaded the first shells into his shot gun. Hawthorne loaded the thrower. He stepped on the pedal and the target launched into the air. With a practiced eye, Rose watched him track the trajectory and fire. The clay target exploded into pieces. He continued, with Rose announcing and marking his score. At the end, he'd successfully hit 23 out of 25 targets.

"Nice shooting, Cowboy," she said as they changed places.

Tate took the paper and winked at her. "I can't wait to stay home and watch Nascar on my free Saturdays."

"Cartoons, maybe," Rose retorted.

Tate responded with a spot-on impression of Bugs Bunny that had her holding her side.

A few deep breaths steadied her nerves and Rose checked her gun and glasses. She nodded at Hawthorne to make sure he was clear of the thrower and steadied her gun against her shoulder, looking straight down the barrel. As she stepped on the pedal, her eyes zeroed in on the small orange target. She squeezed the trigger and felt the impact against her shoulder. The target exploded and she felt a surge of satisfaction.

From there, Rose found her rhythm. Reload, ready, step, fire. She missed a target in the middle of the round and shook her head in frustration. She glanced at Tate, but he gave no taunting smile, just nodded at her as if to say, "You got this."

With two shots left, Rose knew that if she missed one, it would be a tie. If she hit both, she would win.

Rose stepped on the pedal, and a broken target sputtered from the thrower. She released the breath she'd been holding and waited for Hawthorne to reload it. Her foot depressed the pedal again, and Rose followed the path of the target with her eyes and gun. Squeeze.

The target didn't explode, but the impact knocked it off course. She turned back to Tate, waiting to argue why it wasn't a loss.

She raised her eyebrows at him. "You hit it," he affirmed. Cheers rose from bystanders.

She rolled her shoulders back, releasing the tension from the confrontation she had expected. Okay then. One more to go.

She hit the next target cleanly and turned back toward Tate with a smile. His dark eyes held a hint of playfulness and a touch of pride.

He shrugged, acknowledging his defeat. "24 out of 25 beats my 23."

"You know where the shovel is," she replied smartly.

he day felt incredibly warm for May, which might have had something to do with Tate's current location. He was in the middle of the pig pasture, a hundred yards from the nearest source of shade. And he was digging a hole.

He'd ignored two calls from his brother already today, which probably didn't help his mood. Travis just wouldn't leave him alone. Why was he dogging him after all these years? Tate had made himself perfectly clear that their relationship was over when he left home.

He marked out the dimensions with the fluorescent spray paint and cleared the biggest rocks he saw. Wiping the sweat from his forehead with his arm, he decided it was time for a break. There was a patch of trees near the fence where he'd stashed his insulated jug of ice water. He headed toward it while glancing around and pulling off his shirt. The tightness and heat radiating from his neck and arms were telltale signs of a new sunburn. He trickled the chilled water onto the shirt and laid it across his neck as a cooling cloth.

He hung the shirt on the fence to dry and returned to his half-finished hole. Stupid pigs would turn anything into a toy and had managed to dig up and tip over the previous water tank. So Rose was installing a new one. Or he was, thanks to his misplaced confidence in his shooting skills over hers.

He dug most of the hole using the skid steer, but he measured the width and rounded the edges for the circular tank, then pushed it into place and began burying the base so the hogs couldn't dig under it. He'd learned from Rose that the tank had to be deep enough to prevent them rooting under it, and tall enough to keep them from climbing inside and getting their drinking water dirty.

It was a good thing he really liked bacon.

By the time he'd filled in the dirt around the edges of the tank, he was hot and sweaty again. At least he was done. He returned to the trees to grab his water and shirt, but there was no shirt to be found. What in the world? Maybe it had blown away. He checked the trees, and there was no wind today. So much for that explanation.

A flash of red caught his eye. His water cooler was a good thirty yards away from where he'd left it and covered with dirt and dings. He glanced around the pasture, then spotted the hogs not too far away. A piece of white fabric caught his eye, and he groaned. Tate walked toward the fabric on the ground and found his shirt.

Or at least what was left of it.

"Unbelievable," he muttered as he marched back to the skid steer to head in.

He parked the equipment under the overhang and stepped inside the barn. It was marginally cooler in there, and he stopped to enjoy the airflow from the large fans. He stood in front of one and closed his eyes as the air rushed over his face and chest.

"Well, hey there, Cowboy."

His eyes flew open at Rose's voice and heat returned to his cheeks, though from embarrassment this time.

"Uh, hey. One of your pigs ate my shirt."

Rose snickered. "Whoops."

"Yeah. But your tank is in. It's filling up now, probably take thirty minutes or so and then someone should go shut it off."

"I can handle it," she said. "Any other trouble?"

He shook his head and crossed his arms. Her eyes followed the movement and Tate flexed his muscles. Her gaze flew to his, and he smiled as the pink rose to her cheeks.

"Sorry," she offered with a nervous laugh. He liked that he made her nervous. He shouldn't like it nearly as much as he did.

He took a step toward her. Typical Rose—she didn't retreat. Always up for a challenge. The anticipation made his blood race. This was a very bad idea. He couldn't seem to mind though.

"I've missed you," he said quietly, barely loud enough for her to hear.

She swallowed and watched him slowly cross the space toward her. His baseball hat was dark with water or sweat, and his upper body was smooth and muscled, his forearms slightly darker with the start of the season's farmer's tan. "I've missed you too."

"Strange how we can live together and not see each other." He raised an eyebrow, and Rose knew her new morning routine hadn't been as subtle as she'd hoped.

"I've been busy," she said, but the excuse sounded lame even to her. Tate was close now. She could reach out and touch his arm if she were brave enough. His forearm rested on the doorframe, and he looked down at her. She had flashbacks to her bedroom doorway.

"Did we make a mistake?"

"By kissing?" she choked on the words, her throat dry and her blood pressure creeping higher.

"By not doing it again."

The only response Rose could muster was a garbled "mm-hmm" and a head nod. Then Tate's lips were on hers, and she was flooded with the sense of relief and belonging, as though she was finally home after a long trip. Tate smelled like warm dirt and salt. She laid her hand on his arm and pressed up to be closer, to take more.

Her body hummed with approval as he accepted the invitation. The sound of a clearing throat behind her made Rose pull back, only to find the raised eyebrows and crossed arms of her brother watching them.

Her cheeks flushed and she stammered, "We—we were just..."

"Yeah, I saw you 'were just.' Can't say I saw that coming." Hawthorne shook his head and gave Tate a stern look. "My office, now. And put on a freaking shirt."

Hawthorne walked away, and Rose dissolved into mortified laughter. "I'm so sorry, Tate. You could probably just blow him off."

Tate smiled and kissed her gently, giving her tingly feelings in her stomach. "It's okay. It'd be good for us to talk."

"Fine. But I'm a grown woman who makes my own decisions. Don't let Hawthorne go trading goats and gold for my hand or anything."

Tate chuckled and wrapped her in a hug. "The goats all belong to you anyway."

When Tate departed, Rose was left feeling all jittery. She was tempted to go eavesdrop at the door of Hawthorne's office, but she told herself she was overreacting. It wasn't ideal to have been caught making out by her older brother, especially when Tate was shirtless, but they had done nothing wrong. She definitely couldn't bring herself to regret it.

Their friendship meant the world to her, but

there was more than that between them. Rose wanted nothing more than to fall into his arms. Somehow, he understood her better than anyone ever had. With Tate, she could be vulnerable and know he still thought she was strong. It was an intoxicating feeling to be respected and cherished.

TATE GRABBED a shirt from his truck and pulled it over his shoulders. He ran his fingers through his hair and pulled his cap down snugly before knocking on the frame of Hawthorne's office door.

"You wanted to see me, sir?"

Hawthorne rolled his eyes. "Don't 'sir' me. I might be your boss, but I'm your friend too. And I'm having a little trouble processing what I just witnessed."

"Oh, that? That's called a kiss. Give my condolences to Avery for your ignorance."

A smile tugged at Hawthorne's mouth, and he finally broke. "You smart aleck. I'm serious. How long has this been going on?"

Tate sat back in the chair and sighed. "I don't know, man. I guess it started after the tornado. I just... the thought of losing her made me go a little crazy. We kissed, then we talked and decided we should just stick to friends. But then it was super awkward. Today sort of just happened."

Hawthorne raised his eyebrows. "So you're not together?"

"I don't know. I was thinking we would have that conversation, except my boss demanded I come to his office and we didn't get the chance."

"Don't blame me for this. The two of you shouldn't have been doing *that* unless you'd made some decisions, you know?"

A twinge of guilt spread through him. Tate ran a hand over his beard. "Yeah, I know."

"Don't make me go all big brother on you."

"And what do you call this?" Tate raised an eyebrow at his boss.

"Concerned employer. Do I need to add a no fraternizing policy to the employee handbook?"

Tate grinned. "We have an employee handbook?"

"Do I need to create an employee handbook?"

Tate laughed and shook his head. "It's all good. I'd never do anything to hurt Rose, okay? We'll figure it out. Just let us take it at our own pace."

"How long have you worked here?"

"Four years? Why?"

"If you keep going at your pace, I'll retire by the time the two of you figure things out."

"Very funny." Tate stood. "We all good?"

Hawthorne nodded. "I guess. But, Tate?"

"Yeah?"

"She's my little sister. If this goes poorly, you know who has to go."

Tate nodded. Don't overlook that little complication. There was no question about the outcome if he and Rose didn't work out. This was Bloom's Farm. And though he felt like part of the family most of the time, the truth was he would be the pariah. Outcast. Exiled.

Was it worth the risk?

That night, his brother called again. Tate's thumb hovered over the red button for a moment before he answered it. "This is Tate."

"I thought maybe I had the wrong number." His brother's smarmy tone made Tate regret answering.

He kept his tone disinterested and his words clipped. "Nope, still me."

"That's good. Because Dad says you need to come home."

A snort of derision escaped before he could stop it. "Yeah, that's not going to happen." Then, without waiting for a response, Tate hung up the phone and blew out a breath. Ten years and he'd never been back. Nor been invited. There was nothing that could have changed to make him want to go back now.

or the first time in two months, Rose went upstairs the next morning to get her first cup of coffee. As expected, Tate was there at the kitchen table, already enjoying his own.

"Morning, Cowboy."

The bright smile he gave her did more to waken her senses than the caffeine in her hand.

"Will you go on a date with me tonight?"

She raised her eyebrows. "Um, sure?"

"Don't sound so excited," he replied dryly.

"Sorry, you just caught me off guard. What time?" Her mind was racing with the fact that not only had she kissed Tate yesterday, but he'd asked her out on a real date. Her list of things to do today suddenly dropped in importance to make room for this new information.

"I'll try to be done by six. So maybe seven?"

"Sounds good."

That night, Rose waited for Tate in the living room, where her mother and father were settled in with their after-dinner books and newscast.

Tate emerged from the hallway, freshly show- ered and dressed. A button-down shirt with the sleeves rolled up did wonders for his forearms.

"Hey, sorry to make you wait. I thought that was usually the woman's job," he teased.

"Watch it, mister, or I'll make sure to take my time next time."

"Next time, huh?"

Rose flushed. She definitely hoped there was a next time.

Tate waved at her parents. "Keith, Laura, have a good night. We'll be home by ten."

"Have fun!" Laura's cheery voice betrayed her excitement, despite her casual demeanor.

Tate opened the truck door for her, and she climbed inside. When he started the truck, she reached over and turned on the seat warmer.

"It's 70 degrees outside," he commented.

She shrugged. "Then don't turn yours on." He just shook his head.

The cabin of the truck was filled with the woodsy, spicy scent of his cologne. Had he ever worn it before? She couldn't remember.

They talked about their day, and Tate told her about the latest drama on the Minden Farmers' Market committee. Apparently, the lady selling jewelry kept setting up her table too close to the woman selling jelly, and it was causing quite a stir. Rose laughed at Tate's storytelling and before she knew it, they were turning off the highway and onto Main Street in Minden.

Tate parked in front of B&J Bistro before jogging around the front of the truck to open her door. She flushed with pleasure. Around here, it wasn't uncommon for men to open doors when it was convenient. But she'd never had one open her car door.

She stepped into the restaurant first, and the scent of garlic and herbs tickled her nose. She breathed it in deeply. Norm must have something special cooked up tonight. Her mouth watered at the thought. She knew Chrissy, the owner, because she was friends with Daisy. When Chrissy had taken over the small café her parents owned, she'd turned it into a local favorite —the perfect combination of upscale and casual dining for the small-town and surrounding area.

The hostess led them to a table against the wall, and Rose sat on the bench. "I haven't been here in ages. This is perfect."

"Good. I've been here once or twice, but I'd much rather come to Minden than drive to Terre Haute, you know?"

Rose smiled. "Terre Haute too big-city for you, Cowboy?"

"What can I say? Montana is pretty rural. I can handle the city, but if I don't have to, it's even better."

"I get that. There is something almost..." she searched for the word. "I don't know, claustrophobic almost about being surrounded by people and buildings."

"Exactly. At least in Terre Haute, it isn't like skyscrapers and townhouses. Can you imagine living somewhere where the only grass existed in designated parks?"

"Right? I went to New York once to visit Daisy when she was a dancer. I was just a kid, but I still remember wondering where people took their dogs to go to the bathroom!" She laughed. "Then I stepped in something unfortunate and realized the answer was literally on the sidewalk."

"No thank you. I'll stick to rolling hills and pastures. And mountains. I much prefer the feel of dirt under my boots than concrete."

Dinner felt effortless with Tate. Which made sense, considering they'd eaten hundreds of meals together. But there was an undercurrent of something different about this one. It was the subtle recognition that this was a Date with a capital D.

As they finished their meals, Rose decided it was time to confront the elephant in the room. "You never told me what you and Hawthorne talked about, you know."

"Oh, well, the dowry was settled at forty goats and seven years indentured servitude."

Rose couldn't help but laugh. "Did you just make a joke about Jacob and Rachel in the Bible?"

Tate shrugged, but his smile was pleased. "Maybe."

"Come on, for real. What did he say?"

"It was no big deal. He wanted to know what was going on, how long. All that stuff."

Rose scowled. "It's none of his business."

Tate laid a hand on hers. "He loves you. He's just trying to protect you."

She grew serious and met his dark eyes across the table. "Do I need protecting from you, Tate?"

"Probably," he said. "But I need protecting from you too."

Her eyebrows furrowed and he continued. "I care about you, Rose. I would love to see where this goes," he gestured between them. "But I'm also really worried. If I screw it up, that's it. I'm done at Bloom's Farm and I have to leave."

"What? No, you wouldn't." The protest was immediate and intense. Tate couldn't leave. That wasn't even an option.

"But I would, Rose. I couldn't stay behind if we weren't together, not if I hurt you or was hurt by you. Not after knowing what it was like to kiss you and hold you."

Rose stared at his hand on hers. His hands were strong, rough from the hours of work. Not so different from her own. Her fingertips curled up to trace his knuckles. "You already know what it's like to kiss me and hold me." The statement was quiet and a hint of sadness laced her voice.

"Yep. If you don't want to give us a shot, Rose—if you don't feel the same way I do, then I'll probably move on. Maybe not this month, but eventually."

"If I don't feel the same? You haven't really told me how you feel, Tate."

He sighed and scratched his beard. "Rose, I never thought I would consider being with anyone. My mother was such a wreck, partly because of her own demons and partly because of my dad and the ranch. They weren't good for each other. Running the ranch beat my father down. He was a miserable man and made everyone around him miserable too. It's why I left. I didn't want to turn into a mean, angry shell of a man like him. I loved the ranch, but I couldn't handle him."

Rose listened carefully, trying to understand where exactly this was going. It wasn't exactly a declaration of love.

"All that to say, I never expected you, Rose. I never expected a woman so perfectly suited to the life I'd always wanted. I never imagined the possibility that two people could be partners instead of opposing forces. And I definitely never dreamed the thought of leaving someone behind would make me sick to my stomach. I can see a future with you I never thought I would want. I care so deeply for you I'm willing to put all my baggage aside to see if we can make it work. And for the love of football, I want to kiss you again so badly, I can barely function."

Rose laughed and sniffled, her nose and eyes watering at his sweet words.

"So, please—put me out of my misery and say you'd like to give it a shot too."

TATE WATCHED, every muscle in his body tensed and his breath seized in his lungs, waiting for Rose's response. Her hand turned in his, and her fingers traced his palm.

"I never expected you either, Cowboy. I'd really like to see what happens. I'll admit, I'm worried about losing our friendship. I'm worried that you'll change your mind and I'll have lost the best part of my days. But I'm more worried that I might miss my shot at the perfect guy."

Tate's mouth twitched. "You think I'm the perfect guy?"

She rolled her eyes. "Don't get a big head. I just mean we make sense and that maybe it's worth the risk."

"Okay then. Wow. We're doing this."

"Yep, we are."

"I've got to call Hawthorne."

Rose frowned. "What? Why?"

"Sign the paperwork for the goats and all that," he joked. Rose raised an eyebrow. "Just kidding. I want to see about getting an apartment."

"Why?"

He knew he had to explain. "I can't live at the house with you and your parents if we are in a relationship. For one, it doesn't look good. And two, the idea that you are only steps away late at night is wreaking havoc on my sleep." It was entirely true. Last night, he'd tossed and turned for half the night, tempted to do something foolish like walk down the stairs to the basement.

Rose's cheeks turned a delicious shade of pink. "Oh. I could go stay at Poppy's house or something."

"I appreciate that, but it's time for me to get my own place again. Probably one without wheels this time."

Rose didn't say anything, and not knowing what she was thinking was killing him.

Finally she squeezed his hand. "I'll miss our morning coffee chats."

"We can still have them. Just not in our pajamas," he said with a smile.

15

*T*ate moved out two days later, and Rose immediately missed his presence in the large house. Friday night, Tate stopped by the barn before he left work to head back to his rental house in Minden.

"Are you sure we can't hang out tonight?"

He groaned. "I wish we could, but if I don't spend some time unpacking, I won't have any under- wear tomorrow."

She laughed and gave in. "Fine. What about brunch tomorrow? Are you coming?"

Tate's brow wrinkled. "I figured I wasn't on the guest list anymore since I don't live there."

Rose smoothed the end of her braid. "Well, that's true. You don't live there anymore. But we are sort of dating, right? That means you're back on the list. If you want to be," she added.

Tate stepped close. "In that case, I will see you tomorrow morning. Because we are definitely more than 'sort of' dating." With those words, he leaned down to kiss her. Rose knew she probably stank of horses and sweat, but Tate didn't seem to notice. He pressed her against the metal railing of the cattle pen and by the end of the kiss, Rose was abundantly clear on the fact that they were one hundred percent 'definitely' dating.

Brunch in the morning was the usual chaotic gathering of siblings, grandkids, and in-laws. When Tate knocked on the front door, Rose jumped up. "I'll get it!"

"Where's the fire?" Hawthorne asked as she jogged past him.

She opened the door and wrapped her arms around Tate for a hug before welcoming him inside.

They walked into the kitchen. Hawthorne was the first to notice, which was surprising at first, but then Rose realized he had more of a heads up than anyone else.

"I wondered if you'd be here this morning, Tate."

"Why wouldn't he be?" Daisy asked.

"He moved back into his own place," Hawthorne explained.

"Oh, well, surely that doesn't mean he can't come to brunch..." Daisy trailed off, then glanced back and forth between Rose and Tate. "Oh, OH!"

Rose flushed with embarrassment. Tate grabbed her hand and squeezed it lightly. She relaxed at the contact. Her family might be embarrassingly involved with each other's lives, but she could handle it if Tate was there with her.

"So, you two are, like, together now?" Daisy asked with bright eyes and an excited smile.

Rose nodded.

Lavender walked over for a hug. "That's awesome!" Rose dropped Tate's hand to embrace her sister.

"We're so glad you're here, Tate." Laura spoke from her spot at the stove where she was tending the large griddle for pancakes. "How is your new place?"

"It's great. Norm and Miss Ruth seem like great people, and the little cabin I've got is perfect for me. Plus it's tucked back in the woods, which I love."

"You're renting from Miss Ruth?" Rose hadn't realized that Tate's new place in Minden belonged to Miss Ruth. Everyone in Minden and the surrounding counties knew the kind, older woman.

When they'd all gone to church in Minden, Miss Ruth had been their Sunday school teacher. As they'd gotten older, she and her siblings had opted for the more modern, larger church in Terre Haute.

"Yeah. She mentioned that she'd love to have both of us over for dinner one night."

"That's so sweet. I'm up for it, if you are."

"So, Tate, summer is almost here. How's the season look so far?" Rose rolled her eyes at Poppy's question. No surprise that her sister would ask about that. It was probably killing her to be away from the farm so much.

"It's going well. Everything should be out of the greenhouse and into the ground in the next couple of weeks. Then I'll start the fall seeds. Farmers' markets seem to be off to a good start."

"It's not too much for you, is it? Do you have enough help?" Laura asked with a hint of concern.

Tate smiled. "Thank you for asking, but I think we've got it handled. I've got a good team working for me this year."

"Well, if that changes, be sure to let us know."

Instead of listening to her mother and Poppy bug Tate about everything on the farm, Rose made her way to the coffee pot and poured two cups.

Lily stepped up next to her. "Hey, stranger."

Rose turned and gave her sister a hug. "Hey yourself. I feel like I haven't seen you in ages. Everything okay?" She didn't specifically ask the question she was thinking, but with Lily's history of cancer, it was always in the back of her mind.

"Everything's good," Lily replied with a good-natured smile. It probably got tiring to have everyone concerned about you all the time.

"Where's Josh this morning?"

"He's got a wedding to shoot today, and it's all the way down in Bloomington. He left early and will be back pretty late."

Rose could see the disappointment in Lily's face. "Aww, you miss him. You guys are so cute," Rose teased.

Lily laughed. "Yeah, I do. He's my husband, isn't that the point?"

Rose shrugged. "How should I know?" Her gaze drifted across the kitchen to Tate, who was now deep in conversation with Daisy's husband, Lance.

"Oh, I think you have a better idea than you think."

Rose turned back to Lily and saw a knowing smile on her face. "What do you mean?"

"How long have you and Tate been friends?"

"I don't know. Three or four years, I guess."

"And you see each other almost every day, right?"

"I guess so, but that's not the same."

"Sure it is. Maybe not quite the same as Josh and me. But it's a good thing, Rose! I think it's awesome that you and Tate were such good friends before you started dating. Friendship is a great foundation for marriage."

"Whoa there, speed racer. Don't get ahead of yourself. I'm not asking for a reservation at Storybook Barn yet. We just decided to see where this goes a few days ago."

"Just think, the two of you could be the next Mom and Dad. Running the farm, raising a family. It's perfect! Dad will be thrilled."

Rose felt slightly short of breath and felt her heart rate speed up. Lily was just sharing her thoughts, she didn't know Tate and Rose well enough to say anything like that. And she definitely couldn't realize how much the thought of her and Tate becoming her parents was exactly what she didn't want. She'd been fighting to prove for years that she could be trusted to take over the farm.

She'd never assumed that having a husband would be a part of that qualification process. But was Lily right? If she and Tate ended up together and got the farm, would it be because of him, instead of her own accomplishments?

TATE NOTICED Rose seemed distracted at brunch, but it was probably just the adjustment to everyone in the family now knowing about their relationship. It couldn't be easy to navigate that kind of involvement from so many.

At least Tate didn't have to worry about that. He hadn't heard from his brother again since their last call. Which was fine with him. Whatever his dad suddenly thought was so important, Tate wasn't interested. He hadn't even taken the time to call himself, instead he had Travis make the call, like some sort of personal secretary. Typical Steve Russell, too preoccupied with anything else but the people in his life.

Living offsite was proving to be remarkably inconvenient though. As the growing season approached its peak, Tate spent more and more time managing CSA baskets, farmers' markets, greenhouse transplants, and fertilizer applications. The hour he spent in the car each day was time he'd have much rather spent with Rose.

He pulled up in front of the large barn and climbed out. The sun was just peeking above the horizon, and his boots were damp with dew when he stepped inside. He glanced at his watch. Quarter to six. Even Rose, early riser that she was, wouldn't be stopping by for coffee for another hour. There was plenty he could get done before she arrived though.

The next time he looked at the clock, it was after eight. He was elbow deep in the inventory and packing process for the weekly CSA baskets. He'd already been out for a walk through the fields to check the progress of their lettuce, onions, and celery. Tate muttered under his breath and pulled out his phone.

RB: Saw your truck but couldn't find you for coffee this morning.

There was a sad face after the message, then a follow up.

RB: Lunch instead?

He blew out a breath. Tate hated disappointing Rose, and while it wasn't an official date, coffee in the mornings had sort of become their thing and he'd totally dropped it. Even worse, he couldn't do lunch either, since he had plans with a supplier.

TR: I'm sorry about coffee. It's already been a crazy

morning. Wish I could do lunch, but I can't today. Dinner tonight?

RB: Youth group tonight.

Tate tried not to be disappointed. He thought it was great that Rose had volunteered with the church youth group for so many years. It would be selfish of him to, just this once, wish she didn't have to.

TR: Tomorrow night?

RB: It's a date.

Tate slid his phone back into his pocket and went back to counting onions. Tomorrow night seemed like a long way away, but he knew there were plenty of things to keep him busy. It would go by in a flash.

While the representative from the fertilizer company prattled on about the latest and greatest developments in organic fertilizers, Tate's phone rang loudly.

"Sorry about that," he said as he pulled it out. If it was the farm, he could probably wrap things up here. Lunch was over, but the guy just kept talking.

It wasn't the farm though. His brother's name and number flashed on the screen. Tate silenced the call and set the phone face down on the table.

"Do you need to get that?"

"Nope, go on. What were you saying about the expected yield?"

That nudge was all the sales guy needed to go on for another ten minutes. Tate's phone buzzed a few times, but he refused to check it. Travis would give up eventually.

YOUTH GROUP that night was a celebration for the graduating senior class and the end of the school year. As an adult, it always felt nostalgic. When you worked year-round, there was no such thing as summer vacation. Especially on the farm, since summer was one of the busiest seasons. Between the added work for everyone to help with the produce and the extra work keeping the animals watered, fred, and vaccinated. Not to mention the sheep shearing, hay baling, and the petting zoo.

Clearly, Tate had the same issue. They usually saw each other every day, so today had been a letdown. She'd hung around his office and looked around the barn a bit, but Tate had disappeared. She knew better than anyone that an unpredictable schedule came with the territory. After all, hadn't she and Tate bonded over middle-of-the-night deliveries? Still, it was no wonder she hadn't found much time to date before.

At least Tate understood. Why wouldn't he? He grew up on a ranch. And if they stayed together, he'd be as much an owner of Bloom's Farm as she would. Maybe more, if she was supposed to be her mother in this scenario.

The more she thought about her sister's offhanded comments, the more it drove her crazy that all her hard work didn't really matter. All her dad needed was for one of his daughters to marry someone who could run the farm. So much for Hawthorne trading goats for her hand in marriage. Her dad would sign over the farm!

She took a deep breath. Rose knew she was being ridiculous. There was still a lot more to the picture. Hawthorne was happy running the farm, even if he didn't have the day-to-day patience for the fine details.

Still, it still irked her that she wasn't even officially a manager at Bloom's Farm. Wasn't that embarrassing? For five years, she'd been doing everything centered around the livestock, and she was still earning the same amount as she made when she moved back to help her dad. And her father was still looking over her shoulder just as much as he always had.

As she sulked, Pastor Stephen stood up in front of the group of rowdy teenagers and got their attention. After congratulating everyone, he gave a short sermon on spiritual gifts and God's purpose. Rose knew it was aimed at the students, all desperately trying to figure out what they were supposed to do with their lives. But as she listened, her thoughts circled around her own life. She'd never questioned what God had called her to do. It had always been the animals, even when she was a little girl. She loved caring for them, healing them, and sharing them with others. Eventually, she recognized how God had gifted her specifically for those things.

And yet, was it enough? Maybe she wasn't as good as she thought she was. Her dad and brother still seemed intent on involving themselves in every major decision about her animals. She apparently wouldn't get to take over unless she had a man in her life.

It was all so frustrating. And she didn't blame Tate, she really didn't. He was the one who always trusted her expertise and was happy to follow her lead. When he gave suggestions, they came from a place of experience and respect.

She didn't need him. She didn't want to be her mother, as much as she loved her. Laura had helped her dad run the farm, but mostly by keeping the books and occasionally helping with a few chores. But the farm? It was Keith Bloom's. Everyone knew it.

Rose wanted to use the gifts she had been given. She wanted to make it on her own. The last thing she wanted was to finally get everything she'd worked for, but for the wrong reasons. And anything that had to do with her being part of some model future farm family was absolutely the wrong reason.

16

*D*uring the summer, Saturday mornings were reserved for farmers' markets. Tate and his employees divided up the available produce and manned the Bloom's Farm booths at markets from Terre Haute to Greencastle. This week, Tate was in Minden. It helped that he lived there now.

He made change for a customer and shielded his eyes from the sun as he spotted a familiar shape coming toward his table. Rose looked stunning this morning in shorts and a flowy top. Of course, he liked her in jeans and a work shirt, but when she was in anything else—casual or dressy—he sometimes had to do a double-take.

"Good morning, beautiful."

She stepped behind the table with him and kissed him on the cheek.

"Can I interest you in some onions?" he joked.

She smiled. "I think I'll avoid extra onions for now. I wouldn't want bad breath when I go out with my boyfriend."

"He'd probably still kiss you," Tate winked.

Rose laughed, then looked at his half-empty truck bed. "Been busy this morning?"

Tate nodded. Minden was always a good market, but it seemed everyone was eager for some fresh vegetables after the long winter.

"You here to keep me company? To what do I owe the pleasure?"

Rose bagged up an order for a customer while they chatted. "Dad caught me in the kitchen this morning and told me to take the day off. Said he wanted to take care of the chores for once." She shrugged. "Who am I to argue with the boss? Besides, there wasn't much to do this morning. I figured he could handle it."

"It's nice to see how far he's come since the stroke."

"Definitely. There was a time we didn't know if he would walk again, let alone do anything else." Her features were sad and Tate touched her arm.

"What's wrong?"

She shook her head. "Nothing, sorry. I can't help but think how much worse it could have been. Especially since it was my fault."

Tate frowned. "You don't mean that. A stroke isn't anyone's fault, Rose."

Before she responded, Rose rearranged the produce on the table and straightened the small pricing signs. "We had a fight that morning, right before his stroke."

Tate heard the pain in her voice and instinctively wrapped his arms around her shoulders. "That doesn't make it your fault. If arguing with your father could give him a stroke, mine would have croaked a long time ago."

She sniffled a laugh and shook her head. "It's okay. I'm fine. *He's* fine, more importantly. I try not to think about it too much."

"Excuse me, when will you have sweet corn?" The polite question came from across the table, and Tate stepped up to handle the customer.

"It won't be until July, at the earliest. It'll be worth the wait though!" He flashed the woman a smile. "I've got some wonderful asparagus that would be great on the grill," he offered instead. He heard his phone vibrate on the bed of the truck, and nodded when Rose offered to check it. It was probably one of the workers calling from another farmers' market.

"It's Travis?" Rose said, confusion obvious in her voice.

Tate's jaw tightened. "Just ignore it."

Rose raised an eyebrow but silenced the phone. He turned back to the customer and talked her into a bundle of fresh spinach to go with her asparagus.

"Travis is your brother, right?"

Tate nodded curtly. He didn't want to dive into this right now. Or ever, for that matter.

"You can go call him back if you need to. I can handle the booth for a bit."

Agitated, Tate grabbed a crate of broccoli crowns from the back of the truck. Maybe moving something heavy would help him release some of the frustration. "I'm not calling him back."

"Why not?"

"I'm just not."

"He's your brother though."

"Please leave it alone, Rose." He sounded sharper than he meant to. Logically, he knew Rose's question came from the reality of her own experience, where siblings were in constant contact and one another's closest friends. But that wasn't his life.

He wouldn't call his brother back this time, just like he hadn't called him back the last three times he had called.

Rose held up her hands as though in surrender. "Okay, sorry I offered." She stared at him for a second, then turned and walked away from the booth. Of course, all that made him feel like an even bigger jerk. He hadn't meant to take it out on her. She hadn't done anything wrong. Tate sighed and rubbed a hand over his beard.

Really mucked that one up, didn't he? And now he couldn't even follow Rose and apologize because he had to stay and man the table.

Was this how it started for his parents? With a frustrated reaction and no time to deal with it? The hurt in Rose's eyes was exactly the kind of wounded look he remembered seeing from his mother.

"How much is the broccoli?"

Tate was rescued from his thoughts by another customer. "Three dollars each, sir." He would have to deal with it later. Rose would come back eventually and he could apologize. Maybe he could even explain why things were so different for his family compared to hers. Would it help her understand, or would it just make it worse?

AFTER THE THIRD person stopped her to chat, Rose decided small towns were officially unsuited to private pouting. She'd better leave or go back and face Tate. Either way, she couldn't walk around being angry, because too many people insisted on interrupting.

She turned back toward the Bloom's Farm table and came face to face with the familiar smile of Miss Ruth. Her elbow was linked with the arm of a jovial-looking man with gray hair and light blue eyes.

"Rose Bloom, is that you?"

Rose's smile was genuine as she greeted the older woman. "Hi, Miss Ruth. It's good to see you. Norm, how are you?"

"Can't complain."

"Are you here with Tate?" Ruth's question was laced with curiosity and Rose felt the blush in her cheeks in response.

"I did come to see him, but I figured I'd take a lap around the market and check out the competition." That was probably stretching the truth a bit, since she didn't remember a single booth she'd passed. But Ruth laughed at the joke.

"Well, we'll be headed his way soon. Norm has

to decide what the special is tonight at the bistro, but he likes to see what looks good before he decides."

"Best thing a chef can do is let God direct the menu," Norm added.

Rose nodded, "Well, I think we've got some veggies you'll like, but you better head over there soon. Tate has been keeping busy."

Rose made her way back to the table and stood off to the side while Tate completed another transaction. She hadn't been exaggerating to Norm and Ruth about the busyness.

When the coast was clear, she cleared her throat to let Tate know she was there. She stood awkwardly, holding one elbow and unsure of how to approach the situation. She and Tate didn't really fight. Wager, yes. Tease? Absolutely. But fight? Never.

She debated apologizing. It was none of her business whether Tate called his brother back. Obviously, her family was close, but she wasn't naïve enough to think every family was that way. Tate's reaction to her presence made her debate pointless.

TATE STEPPED close and grabbed her hand. "I'm sorry I snapped at you. It's a long story about my brother and my family, and someday, I promise I'll tell you about it. But it doesn't matter—I still shouldn't have taken out my frustration on you. That was a jerk move."

Rose nodded. "It was, but I'm sorry I pushed. Your relationship with Travis is none of my business. It's hard for me to imagine not wanting to answer if one of my sisters called, and I guess I projected that on you a bit."

Tate glanced at a browsing customer before turning back to Rose. "Are we okay?"

"Of course. Oh, Miss Ruth and Norm are headed this way. I guess he wants something for the dinner special at the bistro."

Tate looked at the half-empty truck bed. "I guess we'll see what we've got when he gets here. I should talk to them about pre-ordering. He does this fairly regularly, but I never think to hold things back for him."

"I think that's fair. You'd hate to hold back four bushels of spinach and then be stuck with them."

He stood next to her, leaning against the open tailgate of his truck. Tate watched Rose as she watched the people strolling past the booth. She really was beautiful.

"I really am sorry, Rose."

She looked over at him and gave a small smile. "It's okay." Her fingers nudged his on the tailgate between them, and he shifted his hand to cover hers.

Staring at their linked fingers, he explained. "It's really not. My dad treated my mom like garbage. He took all his frustrations out on her—about the farm, about us kids, about his own bad habits and addictions." Rose squeezed his fingers, and he shifted to meet her eyes. "I never want to be that guy who lashes out at whoever is convenient."

"It really wasn't that bad, Tate."

He shook his head. Regardless of what Rose said, he couldn't help seeing the echoes of his father in his actions.

Before he could say anything, Ruth and Norm walked up.

"Good morning, Miss Ruth. Norm." Tate shook Norm's hand and walked around the table for a hug from the petite redhead.

"Morning, Tate. How are things at the cabin? All good we hope."

Tate grinned. "The cabin is perfect. I feel extremely lucky to have landed there after the tornado wiped out my trailer."

Ruth clucked her tongue and patted his cheek. "You poor thing. God has a way of putting people in that cabin who need it most." She turned to Rose, "And you! Tate here said you were actually in the trailer when the twister hit it?"

Rose nodded sheepishly.

Ruth bustled around the table and wrapped Rose in a hug. "Oh, sweetie. We're so glad you're okay."

"I'm totally fine, Miss Ruth. Thanks to Tate here. Did he tell you he was the one who braved the storm to come get me out?"

Ruth leaned in to whisper in Rose's ear. Tate's whole mood changed at the sound of her laughter. Norm and Tate shifted to talking about the produce and Norm settled on the perfectly ripe asparagus. After hearing the man talk about the ideas he had for using it, Tate's stomach was growling.

"I'm glad I still had enough left for you, Norm. We should chat sometime about reserving what you need instead of hoping you can snag it at the market."

"We could do that. But then I wouldn't have an excuse to bring Ruth here every week for a little morning date."

Tate saw the way Norm looked at Ruth with absolute reverence and adoration. They were a cute couple. "Fair enough," he laughed. "We'll work something out. Someone would have to come pick it up here, even if you've got it reserved."

Norm touched his nose with his forefinger and pointed it at Tate with a wink. "Now you're thinking."

After sending Ruth and Norm off with the asparagus, he and Rose packed up the rest of the booth. The remaining produce would still be good for another farmers' market on Monday evening.

Watching Ruth and Norm together at the market made him wonder about the future for him and Rose. It wasn't the first time. Watching Keith and Laura caused the same longing inside him for a long-term partner. Marriage hadn't worked out for his parents, for more than a handful of reasons. But it was hard to deny the steady, long-lasting love between the Blooms—or the pure, unbridled joy of the older couple who found each other in their golden years.

It wasn't hard to imagine manning the produce table at the farmers' market, a couple of kids counting back change to customers or running off to buy sticks of flavored honey from the beekeeper's table. Or years further down the road, Rose's blonde hair turning to silver, still sharing their coffee at the kitchen table.

His keys smacked him in the chest, and he

rubbed the spot as he bent down to pick them up. Rose was looking at him with barely veiled amusement. "Nice catch, Cowboy," she said with a raised eyebrow.

Tate's smile spread across his face. If the future he imagined included sassy Rose keeping him on his toes, he was on board. He crossed the space between them as Rose continued talking. "If you're back from whatever daydream you were in, I said we're done here. Are you headed back to the farm?"

He turned slightly and gently pushed her against the tailgate of the truck.

"Um, Tate?"

"Yes, Rose?" His fingers traced her collarbone as he tucked his hand behind her neck. She arched her neck into the contact.

"Are you...?" Her words trailed off as he stepped closer and lowered his face to hers.

"I'm going to kiss you now."

Rose's tone was breathy and her eyes drifted closed. "Oh. Okay." The smile danced on his lips before he did exactly as he'd promised.

17

"*A*re you sure you shouldn't talk to your brother?" Rose asked hesitantly after Tate had silenced his call for the second time that week. And that was just while she was around. "It could be something serious."

Tate just jerked a shoulder. "Whatever it is, I'm sure it's fine. Travis has a tendency to make a big deal out of nothing." He turned back to the movie they were watching.

"Okay," she responded, but she wasn't convinced. If she didn't know that Tate would be furious, she would reach out to Travis herself. It wasn't her place though. She'd just continue to pray for him to do the best thing and to not let his emotions drive decisions he might regret. Tate was normally so friendly, generous, and open. But when it came to his family, there was a definite coldness to his behavior. Rose didn't know exactly what hurts lay buried there, but she knew God was the only one who could mend those fences.

She tucked herself closer to his side and tuned back into the romantic comedy. That was one unexpected thing about dating Tate—they never had to fight about what to watch. He was just as content to watch chick flicks as she was.

They were hanging out at the main house tonight, her parents right upstairs. Tate didn't even have a TV at the cabin, so that made it an easy decision. Of course, she was also well aware that being alone at his house late at night was not a wise choice. Not just because three of her sisters had reminded her of the risk of temptation.

Even sitting here in the dark with her parents upstairs, Rose knew it would be easy to forget there were lines they couldn't cross—even though being together felt as natural as breathing. She felt Tate tip his head down to kiss the crown of her head. She sighed and sank into the embrace and the feeling of security that came with being cared for so thoroughly.

The next thing she knew, the end credits were

rolling and Tate was shifting on the couch. She groaned in protest at the space created between them. He chuckled and kissed her temple. "Time for bed, sleeping beauty."

"I wasn't sleeping," she yawned, though she knew it wasn't true.

"The snores seemed to say otherwise."

That woke her up. She gasped. "I do *not* snore!"

"I hate to break it to you, but you do." Tate's crooked smile had her narrowing her eyes.

"You are messing with me, there's no way!"

Tate dodged the little shove she aimed at his shoulder.

"What?" he said with a laugh. "It was cute!"

Rose buried her face in her hands. "Oh my word. Are you serious?"

She was mortified to imagine Tate, trying to enjoy the movie while she was snuggled up against his side sawing logs. She spared one last glance at him and saw him shaking silently with laughter. He was messing with her, the rascal.

When he saw the dirty look she was giving him, Tate's laughter escaped.

"That was mean, Tate Russell." She tried to sound stern, but she was holding back her own laughter. "I will get you back, you know."

Tate stepped close and wrapped her in a hug. "Oh, I know. I'm counting on it."

With a lingering kiss, they said goodnight and Tate left. It was close to eleven o'clock already and morning chores would come early.

The next afternoon, Rose was opening the petting zoo for the summer. There was a steady stream of visitors all day, thanks to the targeted advertising Lavender had arranged on the local radio stations and on social media.

When a tall man with a cowboy hat and boots stepped out of a compact hybrid, Rose raised an eyebrow. Almost exclusively, visitors to the petting zoo were families with young children. Occasionally a couple with no children would come, but a single man? He stuck out like a cow in the sheep pen.

"Hey there, beautiful." Rose already had a bad feeling about the man, but when he got close, she understood why. He looked so much like Tate, except with a hard edge of anger and attitude.

"Um, can I help you?"

"I'm looking for the man in charge." Rose resisted the urge to roll her eyes.

"I'm in charge," she stated firmly.

The man scoffed a mocking, ugly laugh. "Sure, you are, sweetheart." Her fists tightened. "Look, I'll cut to the chase. I'm looking for Tate Russell. Last I'd heard, he was working here. Of course, that doesn't mean much for someone with a work ethic like Tate."

Rose straightened in surprise at the insult. She bit her tongue, despite the defense of Tate that was practically bursting from her lips. She smiled tightly at the awful man she assumed was Tate's brother. "Let me see what I can find out," she replied noncommittally.

She scanned the petting zoo to make sure everyone was doing okay, then ducked around the corner into the hallway. Rose punched Tate's number and prayed he would answer.

"What's up? Are we still on for tonight?"

She ignored his question. "Tate. Code Red. I repeat Code Red. Your brother is here, and he's looking for you."

There was a silent beat and then she heard steel in Tate's voice when he spoke again. "I'm on my way." The line disconnected almost immediately, and Rose sagged against the wall.

She took a deep breath and prepared herself mentally to walk back into the lion's den. Speaking of which, she needed to focus on the petting zoo customers. When she walked back out, Travis was leaning back against a fence, his boots kicked out in front of him like some cheesy stock photo of a cowboy.

"There you are, sweetheart. I thought maybe you ran off and I'd have to come looking for you."

Rose veered to the opposite side of the walkway as she passed him. "Tate's on his way. I've got work to do. You can wait here."

"I'll do that. Can't complain about the view," he said suggestively. Rose whipped her head around and confirmed that he was watching her walk away without an ounce of subtlety.

How could he and Tate be brothers?

"Hey sweetheart, I'll take a cup of coffee when you get a chance!" he hollered after her, but Rose ignored him.

Another voice came from behind her and cut Travis off in a no-nonsense tone. "She's not your sweetheart—or your maid. You'd do better not to talk to her at all, in fact."

TATE SPOKE CAREFULLY, his tone measured through a clenched jaw.

Hearing his brother disrespect Rose like that had

him seriously considering the ramifications of this conversation ending in a fistfight. His feelings for Rose had only grown stronger as they continued their relationship. Being with her felt as natural as breathing, and the best parts of their friendship only seemed enhanced by the added layers of deeper feelings.

Tate stared down his brother, conveying the seriousness of his words.

Travis held up his hands as though in surrender. "Ooh, touchy. No problem. She's not exactly my type anyway. Too prickly."

Ignoring the urge to defend Rose against his brother's mistaken characterization, Tate glanced at Rose. She was busy helping a young girl bottle feed one of the goats, but her eyes were on him and his brother. As much as he appreciated her concern, he needed to get Travis away from the petting zoo.

"Let's go for a walk," he said. Once they were safely away from listening ears—Rose's or otherwise, Tate turned to his brother with resignation. "What are you doing here?"

"You wouldn't take my calls. Figured the only way I was going to talk to you was coming out here myself."

"Maybe that should have been a sign I didn't

want to talk to you, but you never could take a hint."
They continued walking along the fence.

"Is that any way to treat your brother?"

Tate stopped abruptly and turned to face Travis.
"Are you serious? You want to play that card?"

His brother just looked away with a stubborn set
to his jaw.

Tate shook his head. "Okay. Let's talk about how
we treat a brother."

Tate paced again, his agitation making it impossible to stand still. "All those years, I thought we
were on the same team. Dad drove us both hard,
made our lives miserable in high school. No matter
what, it was never enough. But we had each other,
didn't we?" At least, that's how it had started. When
their mom died, Tate and Travis had leaned on each
other.

Tate sighed before continuing, shaking off the
memories of when they'd been closer. "Until we
didn't. Travis, I would have done anything for you. I
don't know what made you think I was the enemy,
but instead of taking ownership of your own
mistakes, you threw me under the bus with Dad
over and over again." Tate still remembered his
confusion the first time he'd been accused of forget-
ting to close the pasture gate, and when Travis had

taken credit for the baling Tate had spent all day doing.

"Then there was the final straw, your accident with the front loader. No matter what I said, he wouldn't hear it. You might have saved yourself a beating, Travis, but you lost yourself a brother that day. I learned the hard way that you are just like him. You'll put yourself first above anyone else, even family."

When Tate finally met his brother's eyes, he saw something that looked like regret. Was it wishful thinking? Then, in a blink, the look was gone. Replaced by a familiar look of contempt. "That's why you left? It was hardly a big deal," Travis mocked. Tate wanted to shake him by the shoulders.

"Hardly a big deal? Your little joyride took out the side of the barn and ruined the bucket on the front loader. I've still got the scars from the lashing I got. Dad sold my horse to pay for the damages, though I'm sure it couldn't have come close to covering it." Tate watched his brother for any hint of a reaction. It had been ten years and the sting of that particular punishment was still surprisingly sharp.

Travis's eyes fell to the floor. "I didn't realize that. You don't understand though. You were the good one—Dad's favorite. I had screwed up so many times, I just knew that one more would set him over the edge. I figured he'd ground you or make you dig ditches." He kicked the dirt with his boot. "Thunder was a good horse."

"He was the best," Tate agreed quietly. Travis had been a dumb kid back then, barely sixteen. Maybe it was time to forgive him. The verses he'd read in Ephesians came to mind, bringing a slight twinge of conviction about the things God had forgiven in his own life.

"Look, Dad's dying, okay?" Travis showed more emotion with those words than he had in the entire conversation up to now. "Doc says maybe six months. And he's been asking me about you, why you never come around, all that."

Tate scoffed. "What'd you tell him? Not the truth, I'm sure."

Travis scratched his beard, a short stubble. "I tell him you're busy. You're happy. All that. He used to act like he believed me when I would say we talked, but he stopped a while back. He wants to see you before he dies. And he wants us to mend fences."

Tate shook his head. "I might think about seeing him, but I'm supposed to just pretend everything is great between us? For what?"

"He says he won't leave us the ranch unless we are on good terms."

"I don't want the ranch." Tate saw the pained expression on his brother's face before he turned away.

"I know you don't. But it's all I've got, Tate. And he won't leave it to just me either. He's talking about selling it and donating the money to charity or some crap like that."

Tate chuckled. "Well, that's different. Since when does Dad care about charity?"

"He doesn't. It's just the best way to spite me if I don't do what he says."

Tate sighed. "So what, I go back to Montana and make nice with you and Dad for a bit so you can get the ranch?"

"Perfect, I'll book your flight."

"Hold your horses. I haven't agreed to anything. What's in it for me?" If he was honest, those verses had been niggling at him since he read them. He was tired of being bitter about his past with his father and brother. Travis's admission of guilt was the closest thing to an apology he was going to get. But he could forgive Travis and not want to be involved with his family or the ranch.

Travis shook his head. "I don't know, man. It was

probably a long shot to even come out here, but I didn't have another choice. Whatever you want, name it."

Tate glanced back at the barn, now several hundred yards from where they stood in the pasture. "I want Mom's wedding ring."

Travis let out a low whistle. "For real? The feisty blonde with the attitude?"

Tate nodded. "Her name is Rose. Learn it."

"Whatever you say."

Tate thought about everything his brother had said. Was he willing to go back and help Travis get the ranch? Facing his dad again was the last thing he wanted.

"What's he like these days?"

Travis seemed to accept the non sequitur and jerked a shoulder. "He's still an S.O.B., but he's mellowed. Probably because he can't kick the crap out of me anymore. The ranch is still the most important thing to him, but I think he's realizing he can't take it with him when he goes."

Tate scratched his beard. "I need to think about this for a bit. How long are you staying?" He started walking toward outside, leading Travis away from Rose and back to his car.

"Flying back home tomorrow."

Tate nodded. "I'll let you know tomorrow morning."

"You've got my number." His brother looked around the farm and then climbed back into the rental sedan.

Tate watched as Travis pulled out and drove away, flooded with thoughts about their conversation. He kept coming back to one question: Was he really going to go home?

18

*R*ose found Tate in the stables, feeding sugar cubes to Mocha and Cappuccino and stroking their noses. She stepped up next to him but didn't say anything. She got the feeling Tate would talk when he was ready.

Nearly five minutes into the silence, Tate finally turned to her. "Sorry. I just needed somewhere to think."

"You're always welcome here. You know that. Do you want to take Capp out for a ride?" A solo ride always helped Rose think more clearly.

He shook his head. "Travis said Dad's sick."

Rose stroked his arm with a sympathetic "Oh."

"He wants me to go back to Montana and help

convince Dad we're on good terms so he'll leave us the ranch."

Tate's low voice held no hint of his feelings on the subject. Rose bit her tongue to hold back her immediate reaction, reminding herself that this was Tate's decision to make. "Wow. What do you think about that?" She knew what she thought, but what about him?

Tate turned to her and she saw the pain in his eyes. "I don't know, Rose. There are a lot of reasons I haven't gone back in ten years. One of whom you had the pleasure of meeting earlier. Part of me wants to tell Travis to pound sand."

Rose hated the bitterness in his voice. "And the other part?"

"The other part is ready to face my old man before he's gone forever. I'm not sure if it would be to make amends or to make sure he knows how much he hurt me. It's my last chance to do either, you know?"

She nodded and wrapped her arms around him. "You don't have to go," she said into his shoulder as they held each other.

"I know." The vibration of his words hummed against her cheek. "What do you think I should do?"

Rose hesitated. Her entire world revolved

around family, and she knew only a fraction of Tate's story. "I think you should go," she whispered. Unspoken, she sent a prayer heavenward that she was giving him good advice.

Tate inhaled deeply, and she leaned back to look at him.

"It might be hard, but I'd be afraid you would regret it forever if you didn't even try."

"I know," he said with a sigh. "Would you. . . do you think you could come with me?"

His dark eyes carried all the vulnerability that question had cost him. Her strong and confident boyfriend needed her to be the strong one.

"Of course." She would need to check with Hawthorne. Having both her and Tate gone would be tough for the farm, but the Bloom family would make it work. Tate was part of the family too.

"Thank you," his voice came in a hoarse whisper. He pulled her tighter, kissing the top of her head.

"It's going to be great," she tried to reassure him. Then she pulled away and smiled broadly. "I can't wait to see where you grew up!" She'd never been to Montana. In fact, she'd never been west of the Mississippi.

"You're going to love it. I might have to buy you a cowboy hat while we're there though."

Rose grinned. "Will you wear one?" She wiggled her eyebrows.

Tate laughed and adjusted his baseball hat. "I don't know. I've gotten pretty used to my ball cap."

"Whatever you say, Cowboy."

FIVE DAYS LATER, Tate drove the rental up the gravel road. At least they'd given him a truck. He'd be laughed off the ranch if he showed up in a hybrid like Travis had in Indiana. Rose sat in the passenger seat, taking in the beautiful landscape and towering Rocky Mountains in the distance.

He soaked in the wide open plain and the rugged, rocky outcroppings. The sky seemed bigger here. Muscle memory took over as he made the final turn that would take them to the ranch. It had been ten years since he made this drive, but it felt like yesterday. Not much had changed. He saw mostly familiar names on the ranch signs they passed, with an occasional new one making him pause.

When they reached the edge of Russell property, he paid close attention. To a practiced eye, it wasn't hard to notice the weathered fences and overgrazed pasture. He tried not to let the worry niggle its way into his mind. It wasn't his ranch anyway. What did he care if they weren't managing things well?

About a mile down, Tate pulled off the county road and onto the rutted ranch drive. The Russell Ranch brand was displayed proudly on the sign over the entrance, a double R.

"Home sweet home," he said with a hint of sarcasm.

"Last chance to turn around," she said.

It was tempting. But he was here now, and Tate wouldn't be scared off. As much as he'd despised his father, and eventually his brother, he appreciated the life he'd had growing up on the ranch. It had instilled a deep love of the land and the animals that never went away. If nothing else, it would be therapeutic to be back here where it all started. If only to say goodbye for good.

Tate parked the truck in front of the house and tried not to be overwhelmed with memories. He could still remember running up the drive after getting off the bus to see his mom waiting for him on the porch.

But she hadn't been there in a long time.

The house could use a fresh coat of paint, but it looked the same as he remembered. He grabbed the bags from the bed of the truck. Rose was waiting for him near the front bumper and he stepped next to her.

He exhaled deeply. "Are you ready for this?" Despite the slight apology from Travis, he really had no idea what he was walking into here. And he'd been desperate enough to bring Rose into his messed-up history.

"Ready when you are, Cowboy." The nickname was just the reassurance he needed. He squeezed her hand before reaching down to grab the suitcase again.

As they headed up to the door, it opened. Travis stepped out. "Glad you made it. Rose, it's good to see you again."

Tate was impressed his brother had managed to remember her name. Clearly Travis was determined to be on his best behavior. They followed Travis inside and he offered them iced tea.

"Welcome to Russell Ranch," Travis directed his words to Rose and she smiled kindly.

"I'm excited to see the rest of it."

"I'm sure y'all have had a long day, so feel free to put your bags upstairs and get settled in. You're in Tate's old room."

Tate nearly choked on his tea. "Um, we're going

to need two rooms. Or I can take a couch or something."

Travis raised his eyebrow. "Oh. I just assumed... No problem." He recovered quickly. "Is the couch in the living room okay? Sorry, it's just that the guest room is full of boxes and papers."

Tate shook his head. "No, it's totally fine. I should have thought to warn you." He wasn't surprised that Travis assumed he and Rose would share a room. Any semblance of faith from his childhood had been purely performance.

He led Rose up the stairs to his old room. The navy walls and wood furniture were the same as when he'd left, and his high school baseball trophies still lined a shelf above the desk. Tate set down Rose's suitcase. She spun in a circle, taking in the room.

"Is it what you expected?"

Rose laughed. "I don't know what I expected. It's a nice room. Am I going to find a secret journal if I go snooping?"

"No journals. Sorry to disappoint."

Rose stepped close and wrapped her arms around his waist. He tipped his head down to meet her gaze. "Are you doing okay with all this?"

"I am. Seeing my dad will be hard, but I'm really glad you're here."

"I'm glad I'm here, too."

He leaned down and met her lips with his own. He knew, without a doubt, that there was no one he would rather face his demons with. Tate traced his thumb from her temple to her jaw, her skin impossibly soft under his. He tucked his hand around to the nape of her neck and tried to pour all his grateful, anxious emotions into the kiss.

Rose leaned into Tate's kiss, letting the fatigue of travel and the apprehension of stepping into the unknown fade away. She simply allowed herself to rest in the presence of Tate.

Since they'd decided to come, she'd been praying for this trip. He'd grown increasingly quiet as they drew closer to the ranch, despite her attempts to make conversation.

Footsteps echoed in the hall outside the bedroom, and they broke the kiss. Rose stepped toward the desk to examine the trophies along the shelf.

"Everything look okay?" Travis stepped into the room, holding his cowboy hat. She really did want to see Tate in one. The man was nearly irresistible in a baseball hat, but a cowboy hat might literally make her swoon, like a delicate woman in a regency romance.

"It's great." Tate's reply was short, but not unkind.

There was an awkward silence before Travis recovered and cleared his throat. "Okay, well, when you are settled, Dad is at the barn. He's eager to see you."

"Ah, yes. So eager he couldn't even come up to the house when we arrived." Tate's voice had a bite to it that made Rose wince.

"Thanks, Travis. We'll be out soon." She gave Travis a polite smile and shut the door behind him when he left. She would do her best to be a bridge and help Tate reconnect with his family. Travis hadn't made the best first impression on her in Indiana, but she was determined to give him the benefit of the doubt. She turned back to Tate and laid a reassuring hand on his arm. "You okay? He can wait if you need some time."

"No, it'll be better to get this over with. You don't have to come with though."

"If you want me there, I'll be there. If you'd rather handle it alone, I'll be fine on my own."

Tate squeezed her hand. "I guess it's time you meet dear old Dad, then."

Rose swallowed nervously but smiled at Tate. Her own apprehension would bring out Tate's protectiveness, and she didn't want him focused on her.

"Let's do it."

19

*O*n the walk to the barn, Tate gave Rose the five-cent tour, pointing out various land-marks and ranch buildings.

"We've got a shop over there, and that's the bunkhouse. It can house six, but I have no idea if they've got full-time ranch hands living on-site these days or not." It was an odd feeling not to know what was going on around his family's ranch. He felt a twinge of guilt, as though he should have been keeping tabs. He shook it off. His lack of involvement in the ranch was as much his dad and brother's fault as it was his own.

"Obviously, you've got the barn and the stables. Corrals and holding pens extend to the west, and there are about 5000 acres of pasture, plus 1000 more in a grazing lease from the state. At least, there used to be."

"Impressive."

Because he knew Rose would understand the significance, he continued talking about how many cows and cow-calf pairs the ranch ran, and the mix of native plants that made up the rich pasture. He could hear the pride in his own voice.

They stepped into the stables, the pungent scent of horses, leather, and hay welcoming him home. He couldn't help but glance at the stall where his horse, Thunder, had been housed, but the unfamiliar eyes of a chestnut greeted him instead.

"That's Lucy." The gruff voice from behind them nearly made him jump. Tate clenched his jaw and turned to face his father.

"Dad," he said by way of greeting. His dad looked smaller than he remembered. Was it because Tate had grown up or was it the illness causing his father to shrink?

Steve Russell cleared his throat and tucked his hands in his pockets. "It's, uh, good to see you, son."

The way his dad shifted his weight made him look nervous, something Tate wasn't sure he ever remembered.

Rose squeezed his hand lightly, and he shook

himself out of the distracted thoughts. "This is Rose Bloom." He hesitated. How much did he want to share? "My girlfriend," he finally finished. Calling her his friend seemed wildly inadequate. Admitting to his father that he was contemplating proposing wasn't exactly on his to-do list.

His father extended a hand. "Nice to meet you, Rose." Apparently, he could play nice when he wanted to. Good to know.

"Thanks so much for having me. I'm excited to finally see where Tate grew up."

His father's curious gaze shifted back to Tate before returning to Rose. "How long have you known my boy here?" Tate's hackles immediately raised, but Rose seemed unfazed by the question.

"Oh, I guess you came to the farm about four years ago now? Is that right, Tate?"

He nodded, still waiting for the other shoe to drop and this polite small talk to disintegrate into an interrogation or a guilt-trip.

"I'm glad you decided to come back. It's been too long."

Or not nearly long enough. Tate couldn't hold back the words that came next. "Travis said you were sick." If his dad wanted to know why he came back, he wouldn't pull any punches. It was entirely possible that if Steve Russell wasn't supposedly dying, Tate would have gladly avoided him and Travis for another five years.

His father gave a wry smile. "Death and taxes, so they say." He sighed heavily. "It's cancer. Who knew smoking for forty years would kill me?"

"Literally everyone, Dad. Pretty sure I told you that when I was ten and I broke all your smokes in half."

His dad chuckled. "I forgot about that. You destroyed a whole carton, you little punk."

Tate shrugged. "Apparently I didn't want you to die of lung cancer. How dare I?"

"Yeah, well, maybe I should have listened. Doc says I've got six months, maybe less." As though to emphasize the point, his father wheezed the last few words before succumbing to a coughing fit that had Tate wincing.

"Can we get you some water or anything?"

Rose's concerned voice spurred him into action. He led his dad to a bench near the wall, even as Steve protested with a raised hand and a shake of his head through his coughs.

When the coughing subsided, his dad leaned back against the wall. "I'm okay. It's all right."

"You shouldn't be out here working, Dad."

"I'm not an invalid. And the ranch needs me."

Tate resisted the urge to roll his eyes. Of course, his father would assume the ranch would fall to pieces if he weren't there to manage every little thing.

"I'm sure Travis can manage things for an afternoon," he insisted. Then after his father protested some more, he added, "I'll touch base with him and help him out with whatever he needs, okay?"

The next morning, Tate rose early to join his brother for the day. The last thing his dad needed was to be out on the range moving the cattle. Dust and dirt would do no favors for his already fragile lungs. They saddled their horses and headed to the pasture, along with two of the ranch hands.

The ranch hands broke off to come around the south side, leaving Tate alone with Travis. "Are things okay around here?" Perhaps he should have eased in to the conversation, but the subtle signs of neglect were hard to ignore. Rotted floorboards beneath a roof leak in the stable, a broken gate hobbled together instead of fixed properly. A section of fence laid down with enough brush grown up around it to prove it had been down at least a year.

Travis shrugged. "Things are fine. Last year was

a little tight, but we'll make it through. This is the year things fall into place."

Tate tried to analyze the truth of his brother's words. He sounded confident, but was it misplaced? There were no guarantees in the ranching world. What made Travis so sure this year would be better? It was early, still months away from sending any head to auction.

Instead of pushing further, he simply nodded. "Glad to hear it."

"Did you and Dad get a chance to talk last night?"

Tate shrugged. "A little. We didn't get into anything important."

It seemed like maybe Travis wanted to say more, but they reached the herd and needed to split up in order to push the cattle in the direction of the new pasture they had opened. For the next several hours, Tate simply enjoyed the job at hand. As much as he enjoyed managing the produce operation at Bloom's Farm, he truly loved working with the animals. He'd be sore tomorrow after so long in the saddle, but it would be worth it.

He couldn't let his dad get rid of the ranch. Even if it was only to Travis, Russell Ranch needed to stay in the family. For the first time in ten years, he wondered if he'd made a mistake by leaving.

Of course, that would mean he would never have met Rose, which was a sobering and painful thought. He hoped she was doing okay at the house today. She was technically there with his father, which wasn't ideal, but when he'd suggested she come along, Rose had begged off. Knowing her, she probably thought he needed the time alone with his brother.

He saw Travis across the pasture, rounding up a straggling cow-calf pair and urging them toward the rest of the herd. Tate wanted to trust his brother. He wanted to believe that Travis had grown up over the years and that given the opportunity, he would do the right thing when faced with a difficult situation.

But deep in his belly, there was still that hint of unease and mistrust. Travis was too much like his father, perhaps. Too willing to sacrifice people and relationships for money or success. Whether his dad had learned that lesson in his old age remained to be seen.

When they were almost done, Travis waved him over. Looking around the now empty pasture, Tate tried to guess what his brother wanted. They sat tall on their horses and watched the last of the cattle flow through the gate into the newly opened grazing space as flies buzzed around them. A cool breeze danced through the grass and brought a welcome wave of relief from the intense sun.

"Thanks for your help today." Travis's tone was serious and a bit gruff. He cleared his throat and continued, "I'm glad you came back."

The way his brother shifted in his saddle betrayed his discomfort. Tate watched carefully for some sign of the insincerity he expected. There was none, just an honest declaration of appreciation. "I'm still not staying." His words were firm, but in his gut, he felt a quiver of uncertainty. Would he consider staying?

"I know. But it's still nice to have you around. It hasn't been the same without you."

"You're just tired of dealing with Dad on your own," Tate remarked with a smirk.

"Well, that's true. You see how he's different though?"

He gave a thoughtful nod. "Yeah. He seems tired." The man had worked nearly sixteen hours a day Tate's entire life, and now even the lightest ranch duties took him hours to recover from.

Travis stared over the rolling hills. When he spoke, Tate heard the emotion in his voice. "I just want to make him proud, you know?"

Oh yeah. He knew. Tate had spent the first eighteen years of his life trying to earn the approval of his father. Apparently, he had learned the lesson that Travis never had. Nothing was good enough for Steve Russell. A wave of sympathy for his brother came over him. The best thing Tate had ever done was leave the ranch and the toxic influence of his father. Travis, on the other hand, had stayed and dealt with it every day for a decade.

"I'm sorry, Travis. I'm sure he is, even if he doesn't express it."

Travis looked at him with dark brown eyes he knew mirrored his own. A quick nod of appreciation, and the moment was gone. "I think we're done here. Want to grab a couple fishing poles and hit the pond?"

Memories of early summer mornings spent on the shores of the small creek-fed pond filled his thoughts. Away from the crushing presence of their father, he and Travis had talked about everything while catching bluegill, perch, and brown trout.

"I'd love to get out there, but I should go back and catch up with Rose. Maybe I'll take her and show her our old stomping grounds." He felt a little guilty for abandoning her. A romantic evening on the dock would be the perfect way to end the day.

"That's fair," Travis said. "She'll love it. Rose seems like a real keeper."

Tate clicked his tongue. "I think so too." He urged his horse into motion with his heels. After a long day working on the ranch, it was time to go find Rose. The anticipation of an evening relaxing with the perfect woman had him smiling the entire ride back to the barn.

20

*R*ose had to admit the dusty, sweaty smell of horse and cattle pasture on Tate was even more enticing than his usual dirt and oil. On the back of the four-wheeler, she clung tightly to Tate's waist. They quickly left the part of the ranch she was familiar with. Wandering around the ranch today without him had been uneventful. She didn't go too far from the house or barn, but she could already appreciate the rugged landscape.

Tate led them down a rutted path along the edge of a pasture. The path slowly climbed, so gradually Rose didn't even realize how high they'd come until he stopped the engine at the edge of a bluff. Wide open country spread out below them and Rose drank in the sight. Mountains rose in the distance, and a broad, winding creek played peekaboo through patches of scraggly trees. Cattle dotted the landscape, comfortably grazing on the open plains.

"Wow," she breathed the word.

"Home sweet home," Tate said quietly. He pointed to the left, "There's the main house and the barn. Our property goes all the way to that ridgeline over there."

"It's incredible." The sky was making the slow transition from bright blue to purple as the sun sank below the horizon. The edges of the clouds were painted with brilliant oranges and pinks and reds.

"I'm glad you think so. I'm sorry I didn't get to spend time with you today."

She shrugged a shoulder. Tate was far more perceptive than she gave him credit for sometimes. She thought she had hidden her disappointment better this morning when he said he was helping Travis. "It's okay. You needed to spend that time with your brother. If there is anything I understand, it's the demands of siblings."

Tate chuckled at her comment. "It was good. We talked a bit and worked a lot. It felt good to be out there again. Feels different to spend the day in the saddle instead of a tractor seat." Twisting in the seat, he pointed behind them to a bramble of bushes tucked in the rock formation. "See those flowers? Those are wild roses. My mom always used to call this spot Rose Ridge."

Rose rested her cheek between his shoulder blades and continued to watch the sunset over Tate's childhood home. She could feel the subtle change in him. It was obvious he loved the land. Despite the tension with his father, Tate seemed just a little lighter here than he did at Bloom's Farm.

Was it just being here? Or was there something else happening with him she couldn't see? Whatever it was, it was refreshing to see Tate talking about his brother without the bitterness that marked the conversations they'd had about him in Indiana.

They sat in silence, the sounds of the night coming alive around them. Tate finally broke the silence, turning his head slightly to speak to her. "When I think of this spot on the ranch, I'll always think of this moment. It's destined to be Rose Ridge."

She felt her heart crack wide open at his declaration. Falling for a rugged cowboy didn't usually lend itself to romantic whispers, but Tate's words had her blushing with pleasure. "I'll never forget this," she replied.

He kissed her gently, and they watched the sky for another moment before Tate grinned at her. "Are you ready for a little fishing in the dark?"

"I was born ready, Cowboy."

AT DINNER THE NEXT NIGHT, Tate sat across from his father. "How are you feeling, Dad?" He looked less tired than he had a few days before—hopefully the day off had given him some much-needed rest.

"I'm doing just fine. Matter of fact, I hear I could run circles around you after you spent all day on that horse yesterday. Rose here tells me you don't saddle up much these days."

Rose gave a guilty smile.

"That's true. I'm more likely to be in a tractor than astride a stallion. But working the farm is pretty amazing. We grow all kinds of crops. I've learned more about vegetables than I ever wanted to know."

"Got any cattle on that farm of yours?" Tate pressed his lips together and tried not to be offended. Of course, his dad would only care about the live-stock. He let Rose respond.

"I manage the animals, sir. We've got about

twenty head of cattle, but we also have hogs, goats, sheep, chickens, and horses."

His father scoffed. "Sounds more like a zoo than a ranch."

"Actually, two years ago I expanded our petting zoo hours. It used to be special events only. It's a huge hit with the kids." Rose beamed with pride and Tate grinned. She'd worked hard to make the petting zoo a special part of a visit to Bloom's Farm. It had made all of their events—the Pick-Your-Own Apple Days, the blueberry picking season, even the pumpkin patch—more successful.

"A petting zoo?" Tate could hear the disdain in his father's voice. "What kind of circus are you working for, Tate?"

"That's enough," he said through gritted teeth. Insulting Bloom's Farm wouldn't go over well with him. Or Rose. He stole a glance in her direction and saw the hurt disguised behind a frozen smile on her face.

"I'm just saying, isn't it nice to be back on a real ranch?"

Tate shook his head. "You don't get it. Bloom's Farm is more than just a farm. Yes, it's a business. But it's a family. It's a staple in the community. It's a petting zoo and a bed-and-breakfast. And a produce stand at the local farmer's market."

Rose squeezed his hand under the table. "I think what Tate is trying to say is that there is no use comparing Russell Ranch with Bloom's Farm. They are completely different, and that's okay. It's fascinating for me to see the operation you have. It's an entirely different level than anything I have dealt with. Have you ever had other animals on the ranch?"

With her question, Travis and his father were off on a tangent about how they'd tried sheep once but couldn't get the hang of it. Tate laughed as Travis told the story about attempting to learn to shear the sheep himself before finally hiring professionals.

"Oh yeah. Hiring professionals is definitely the way to go, unless your flock is huge."

"Yep. So we stuck with cattle. The last few years have been rough, but Travis tells me the batch we've got for auction is likely to be our biggest ever, both in number and weight."

Tate perked up. "Oh, why so large?"

Travis shrugged and rubbed his jaw. "Not sure exactly. Just a hearty group, I guess."

It wasn't lost on Tate that his brother didn't meet his eyes. Was he being suspicious for no reason?

"Well, that's great. I hope it turns out like you expect."

"You going to stick around and find out?" His dad's gruff question had rendered the entire table silent.

Travis tried to jump in, "Dad, I told you—"

"I know what you said. But I want to hear it from him."

Tate swallowed. "I, uh..." He had no idea how to answer that question. The truth was that until five days ago, he hadn't even considered coming back here an option.

"We haven't really discussed it yet." Rose's composed voice settled his nerves.

Tate swallowed and spoke frankly. "I love this ranch, I always have. But I love Bloom's Farm too. I hadn't considered the possibility that I would have to choose between the two."

And if he had to choose between the two, that meant Rose would have to choose between them as well. Unless she wasn't as serious as he was. But he thought she was. They always seemed so perfectly in sync.

"I see. So where does that leave me? I'm a dying old man hoping I'd get to see my sons working together to take over the business I built with my bare hands."

His dad was being pretty dramatic, considering he had inherited a good portion of the ranch from Tate's grandfather. It was a full-force attempt to lay a guilt trip on Tate without an ounce of subtlety. Tate got his point though. His dad was dying. Nothing Tate could do would change that at this point. And he wasn't about to let his dad manipulate him into a decision.

"I don't know what to tell you, Dad. If you want to leave the ranch to Travis, I'm sure he'll take good care of it. If you want to wait and see if I'll come around and be a part of Russell Ranch again? You might be waiting a long time."

Tate stood up from the table and cleared his half-empty plate. The huge appetite he'd worked up on the range was suddenly nowhere to be found. Rose hurriedly did the same. She followed him up the stairs with a polite, "Excuse us," to his dad and brother.

Once they were safely in his old bedroom, Tate paced while Rose perched on the edge of the bed. "Can you believe his nerve? I've been here twenty-four hours, and he disses Bloom's Farm and expects me to give up my whole life to come back for good?"

It wasn't even surprising. His dad had never cared about anything more than himself and his ranch. The idea that Tate would choose something else wouldn't even register.

"He just wants to see his sons working together like he always imagined." Rose's calm, kind words were a sharp contrast to his animated outburst.

Tate pinched the bridge of his nose to ward off a headache. "Gah. I know he does. And he's dying, so I guess that means he gets a free pass on rude comments. He couldn't care less about what I do at Bloom's Farm. Did you notice that? It was like his eyes glazed over when I started talking about produce."

Rose laughed, "To be fair, sometimes my eyes glaze over when you talk germination schedules and harvest timelines." She shrugged apologetically. "Sorry, but it's true. Animals are way more interesting."

Tate pulled an imaginary dagger from his chest. "Ouch, babe. Warn me next time you're going to cut me like that. Also, I'm going to tell Poppy you said that." He felt the smile grow on his face as he enjoyed the easy rhythm of being with Rose.

"You wouldn't dare!" Her eyes grew wide, but her smile revealed her lack of true concern.

He collapsed beside her with a chuckle that morphed into a sigh as he laid back on the bed. Their light banter was just what he needed to decompress after a day with his family. Rose leaned back and they stared at the ceiling together.

"A few more days here, and we'll go back to Indiana," she said.

"Yeah." But the unspoken thoughts of the day wouldn't stop rattling around, begging to be given a voice. "I'm not saying that I do. But what if I wanted to stay?" He still wasn't sure, but despite his dad's attitude, there was something about the ranch that was calling him. He had always loved the land and the work. And if he really could find peace with his family, shouldn't he do that?

Rose sat upright and looked down at him. "What are you saying?"

He leaned up on his elbow. "I'm not really saying anything. It's just that being back here is this strange alternate future I never expected. Being out there today... I remembered how much I loved it. Not the dealing with my father part, but the actual ranching? Yeah, I miss it."

"Wow. I... I had no idea." Rose's voice was detached, unemotional. He'd give anything to know what she was thinking. Without a doubt, he didn't want to do anything without her beside him.

She was his best friend.

His partner.

The person he cared most about in the entire world.

"Hey," he reached a hand up and tucked it along her jawline. Worry creased her forehead and her eyes were shadowed with a hint of sadness. "I'm not saying any of this to make you feel bad or worry. I feel like..." How could he tell her where his heart was? The thoughts he'd mentioned were only half the story. "You should know that I love you, Rose." Her eyes widened in surprise. He kept talking, knowing he needed to say more, with no expectation of a declaration in return. "Right now, any discussion or consideration about my future has to include you. Is that crazy?" He lowered his forehead to hers.

She shook her head. "No, not crazy. And I love you too." A surge of joy filled him at her words. Everything would be okay, no matter what they decided. She wasn't just his best friend. Rose was the woman he loved. And she loved him in return.

Rose laid back down, and he looked down into her eyes. "That's very, very good to know. We'll just figure it out together, all right?" At her soft smile of agreement, Tate leaned down and pressed a gentle kiss to her lips. He would never tire of the way they fit together. He explored her lips and memorized the breathy sighs of contentment she made.

Farm or ranch, didn't matter. Everything that counted was right here in this room.

21

*R*ose couldn't stop replaying Tate's words about staying at the ranch. Even though he'd tried to play it off like he wasn't thinking about staying, it was obvious that there was something in him that was. She could tell by the way he acted at Rose Ridge, or the way he eagerly left with his brother this morning to repair a broken gate in the north pasture.

Montana was calling out to Tate. And Rose didn't know what to do about it. Bloom's Farm was all she'd ever wanted. All she'd ever worked for. Even the slight possibility that Bloom's Farm wasn't in her future had her slightly panicky. But the thought of being without Tate? That was almost worse.

Tired of debating with herself, Rose called her sister Poppy.

"Hey Rosie. How's the wild west?"

Rose smiled at the sound of toddler yells in the background. "It's gorgeous out here. I can see the appeal, but I miss the farm."

"I bet you do. It's not like you to leave the animals behind."

Rose felt a twinge of guilt. "I know, but I needed to be here for Tate."

"Oh, believe me. I understand."

"Actually, that's why I'm calling." Rose hesitated. How could she explain what she was feeling? "I think Tate might want to stay in Montana."

"Oh." Poppy's voice betrayed her surprise.

"Yeah, that's kind of how I feel. I can see how happy he is here, and how much he loves his family's ranch. I just never expected it, you know?"

"Whoa. So... would you consider staying with him? Are you guys that serious?"

Rose blushed, thinking of the warm kisses and sweet words. "Yeah. We're serious." Then, she sighed. "But it's Bloom's Farm. It's home."

"Yes, it is."

"To be honest, of anyone in the family, I always thought it would be me and you running the place in the end." Poppy had been as dedicated to her produce business as Rose was to the animals.

Poppy chuckled. "I did, too, sis."

"So what happened? How could you just leave when you cared so much about the farm?"

Rose briefly heard Poppy talking to Magnolia. "Mommy's on the phone right now. Go play and I'll be there in just a minute." Then she was back. "It was hard. And obviously our circumstances were slightly different, and I'm still close. But in the end, I loved Harrison. I would have gone anywhere to be with him and watch him embrace God's call for his life. And you know, I shouldn't have been surprised that God's calling for me was a perfect match for Harrison's."

There was a lot to think about in her sister's words. "Thanks, Poppy. That really helps. I'm going to go for a walk and pray a bit. Give Maggie and Henry a kiss from Aunt Rose."

They hung up and Rose leaned back on the bed. Poppy made it sound so simple. Was Rose willing to go anywhere to be with Tate? If she wasn't, did that mean she didn't really love him?

She prayed for answers as she meandered around the property, not straying far from the main house. When she'd run out of words for God, she changed course and headed to the barn. Walking through it was disappointing, since all the animals were in the pasture. It was a nice facility though. She wanted to talk to Travis or Tate about the chute system they had for the cattle. It looked like a chaotic maze, but she knew from experience that there was a rhyme and reason to every decision.

Rose found herself in the supply closet of the barn while looking for a broom. She might as well lend a helping hand while she was wandering. Instead of a broom, she found a small closet stuffed with white boxes. She picked one up, turning it over in her hands, trying to interpret the foreign language on the label.

One box was open, the hormone implant disc catching her eye. Shock and horror washed over her as she examined the label. Her heartbeat thundered in her ears and she glanced over her shoulder. Was that someone walking outside? If this was why Travis was so confident in his auction results this fall, she had to do something. But what could she do?

Tate was falling more in love with the ranch with every passing hour. And he and Travis really seemed to be getting along. After the confrontation at dinner, even Steve had lightened up a bit and simply seemed to enjoy having his family back together.

This revelation would devastate Tate, but she had to tell him. Of course, there was no proof. These implants weren't technically in the livestock. But why would they have them if they weren't using them? She knew about Diethylstilbestrol, or DES, from her large animal pharmacology class at vet tech school. The synthetic hormone was banned decades ago because of the cancer-causing residual levels found in the meat products. If Travis and Steve were using DES to bulk up their cattle, they were doing so at the cost of human life.

Her hands shaking, she snapped a few pictures and tucked one of the small packages in her pocket. Sweat beaded at her temples. She needed to think this through, but first, she had to get out of here.

Rose backtracked from the closet and stepped into the hallway. She stopped short at the sight of Travis standing only a few feet away. "Lost, sweetheart?"

Was she imagining the menacing tone of his voice? Or did he know what she'd found?

Her mind raced as she tried to explain. "I was, uh, looking for a broom."

Travis didn't speak, and Rose was debating whether her best bet was to run first or scream.

Finally, he tipped his head to the left. "Just around the corner."

"I just remembered I'm supposed to call my brother back this afternoon." She felt his dark eyes watching her as she scurried past him. Her heart was pounding in her chest and she walked as fast as she dared back into the main house.

Once she was up in the bedroom, she pulled out her phone.

RB: I need to talk to you. ASAP.

She didn't get a reply. Tate was probably off with his dad somewhere, talking water rights and grazing patterns. Rose hung her head in her hands and pressed her palms into her eyes. She started praying for wisdom and how to approach this conversation with Tate. He was going to be devastated. Of course, it meant that he had been right all along. She was the one who had pushed him into coming back.

A knock on her door made her jump, and Rose quickly tried to calm her racing heart. She cracked the door to find Travis waiting for her.

"I figured I should talk to you about what you saw in that closet."

Rose gathered her courage and spoke firmly. "That's okay. I know what I saw, and I'll just talk to Tate about it later."

"Oh, well, that's fine. I told him about the DES yesterday when we were talking about the herds. You know, trying to save the family ranch and all. You do what you gotta do." Travis was cool and collected, as though he couldn't care less if she told Tate.

Rose pulled back. "Including killing people? There is no way Tate would be okay with this." Not the man she knew. He would never do something illegal and dangerous just to earn an extra buck or two.

Travis held up his hands. "Whatever you say. But he was totally understanding when I told him. Family is the most important thing, right?" With that, he turned away.

Rose simply shut the door to the hallway and locked the door. She paced the small room, surrounded by Tate's high school trophies and photos. Travis had to be lying.

After a few hours, when Tate still hadn't returned, Rose knew she couldn't continue hiding in the bedroom. Once in the hallway, the sound of voices drew her downstairs.

Travis's words reached her as she approached the bottom step. "Are you sure you're okay with this? I figured you for a rule-follower." Were they talking about the DES? She quickly descended the remaining steps, eager to enter the kitchen.

"Yeah. Why wouldn't I be? Some things are more important than blindly listening to authority." Tate's response froze her in her tracks. This couldn't be happening.

She peeked around the corner and saw Tate sitting across from his brother at the kitchen table, his back to her. Travis's eyes flickered at her appearance, but he gave no other indication she was there. Tate had no idea.

"Like family?" Travis's dark eyes were locked on his brother and Tate nodded. The implications raced through her head.

"Exactly." Travis had said the same thing upstairs. Did Tate really believe his family was more important than doing the right thing? Even after so many years away from them?

"I'm glad. Four years is a long time. Are you surprised no one ever suspected?"

Four years? So this wasn't a new foray into DES. Travis and Steve Russell were past the point of no return now. The cattle they would have butchered this year would have trace amounts of carcinogens in them.

"People ignore what is under their nose all the

time. This is the right thing to do. For us. For the future." Rose's heart sank at Tate's words. Tate was complicit in the illegal doping of cattle. What more evidence did she need? Travis hadn't lied. She looked again at Tate's brother. His face was a harder, leaner version of Tate's and he returned her gaze for a moment before refocusing on Tate.

At his words, Rose covered her mouth and sagged against the stairway wall as the implication of the conversation she'd just overheard washed over her.

If she hadn't heard it with her own ears, she never would have believed. She hadn't expected to stumble onto the conversation between Tate and Travis when she was on her way to break the news. But obviously, Travis hadn't been lying. Maybe Tate was more desperate to reclaim his position at Russell Ranch than she thought.

Did Tate really think she would go along with this as well? If he thought she would be okay with it, then he didn't know her at all.

Tate fingered the engagement ring. The simple gold ring and diamond setting had belonged to his mother. His dad might have tried to play it off like he didn't know where the ring was, but Tate wasn't falling for it. Tate had far more claim to the ring than his father did, seeing as his dad was the one to blame for her suicide. Tate wouldn't leave without the ring in his hand. He meant what he'd said about things more important than following authority. Steve Russell might still be his father, but Tate didn't answer to him anymore.

Tate smiled, thinking about Travis's last question. He and Rose had been friends for four years before taking the leap. Had anyone suspected anything between them? If so, it hadn't been him. His feelings for Rose had blindsided him, despite being right under his nose.

"Are you going to tell Rose?" Travis's question broke Tate's silent reverie.

"She doesn't need to know yet. I think she's in for the long haul, but I want to make sure. You know?" This trip had shown him a different side of Rose, proving she was kind and patient, and that he could trust her to help him make good decisions. Rose was like family to him, far more than his father was these days. Travis seemed to understand, even if his father didn't.

Travis raised his glass of sweet tea in a toast. "Oh, definitely. Whatever you think is best, man."

Tate snapped the small, black box shut, hiding the ring from view. He just had to wait until the time was right to talk to Rose and ask her the most important question of his life. Once they'd committed to a future together, they could figure out where that future would happen.

Whether it was Bloom's Farm or Russell Ranch, he didn't really care. Not if his ring was on her finger.

ROSE RETURNED to her room and lay on the bed, staring at the ceiling. She checked her watch. It was late at home, but not too late to call.

"Hey, Rose! How is Montana?" Lavender's voice made Rose's throat burn with the threat of tears. Oh, how she missed home!

"It's fine. I mean, Montana is beautiful." She tried to sound cheerful.

Apparently her attempt was unsuccessful, because Lavender didn't even hesitate. "What's wrong?"

Rose took a deep breath and turned on her side. "I've got a big problem." She explained everything to

Lavender: the illegal hormones, Travis's claim that Tate knew, and the conversation in the kitchen. "I don't know what to think anymore, Lovey. I think I'm going to come home."

"Wow. That's a lot to take in, Rose." Lavender hesitated. "Obviously, you need to talk to Tate."

Rose groaned. "That's what I was afraid of. But what's the point? At best, he's letting his brother give people cancer for a few extra bucks. At worst, he's going to take over the ranch and do the same thing."

"I know it seems bad right now, Rose. But you and Tate have been friends for a long time. He deserves a conversation."

"You're right. I'm just not sure I can handle hearing him say it to my face."

"It'll be okay. But you're a grown woman. You trust Tate, right?"

Rose considered it. She did trust Tate. Maybe this was just a temporary lapse of judgement for him and she could talk him out of it. He just came back to the ranch and fell in love with it all over again. She could understand letting emotions overrule wisdom every now and then.

"Okay, you're right. I'll talk to him." She'd bring it up with Tate, and hopefully, he would see that she only wanted the best for him.

22

*T*ate felt the weight of the ring in his pocket. When the time was right, he would ask Rose to be his wife. The thought sent a thrill of excitement through him. Being back on Russell Ranch had made everything crystal clear for him. He loved Bloom's Farm. He loved the ranch. But neither of them would be enough if he didn't have her by his side.

He hadn't seen Rose all day, so he went looking for her. Tate wasn't the least bit surprised to find her in the stables, grooming and murmuring to one of the horses.

"Feels like we should get you a cowboy hat, hanging around the ranch and all."

Rose's smile didn't reach her eyes when she turned to him. "Hey, Cowboy."

"Everything okay?"

She shook her head slightly, and Tate's mind started racing. Was it something back at the farm? Her family?

He reached out to touch her arm, but she pulled away.

"I have to talk to you... About the ranch."

"Isn't it great here?" He couldn't help but let his own enthusiasm show. He desperately wanted her to love it as much as he did.

"The ranch is great, Tate. But I can't let you do this."

"What do you mean?" Tate's confusion increased with every word she spoke.

"You are letting your brother pressure you into something you don't really want to do."

Tate recoiled. What was she talking about? Was this about staying on the ranch? Maybe he wanted to stay, but it wasn't because Travis was pressuring him. "I'm not letting Travis pressure me into anything. I'm a grown man, Rose. I make my own decisions. Just because I've been living on Bloom's Farm for the past four years doesn't mean that's the only place for me. I thought we were going to figure this out together?" He felt the agitation rise. He was willing to give up everything for her, but he wanted to at least have the conversation. Leave it to independent, strong-willed Rose to have it all figured out without him. "But you've already decided for both of us, haven't you?"

"Wait, that's not what—"

"I should have figured that you'd never give up anything for the two of us. You're not that different from my dad. The farm comes first. I don't know why I'm surprised. I should have realized you've always been like that." He broke into an exaggerated impression of Rose. "Sorry, Tate. I can't hang out; I need to check the hogs. Sorry I'm late; I had to bottle feed a goat. Whoops, sorry I stood you up! The barn was five degrees too cold, and I had to knit blankets for every horse."

Rose's eyes flashed with anger. "I'm sorry I care about my animals and sometimes I have to prioritize them. That doesn't even compare to the messed-up priorities around this place."

Tate stepped backward, unwilling to listen to Rose insult his family and his ranch. "You know what? If you don't like it around here, maybe you should just go home." Her rejection of the ranch stung far more than he thought it would. It felt like she was rejecting him by extension.

Maybe this was inevitable and the reality was that neither of them was ready to walk away from their family business. Right now, he was just angry and sad. The ring in his pocket seemed a cruel reminder of his foolish fantasy of a happy family ending. It would seem Russells don't get happy endings.

"I guess I will." Rose's tone was resigned, laced with sadness.

ROSE HITCHED a ride to the airport with one of the farm hands. Tate didn't even come to see her off. It was a disappointing realization that they'd gone from declarations of love to near-total indifference in just a matter of days.

The trip back to Bloom's Farm seemed to take hours longer than the trip to the ranch. Was it simply the absence of Tate as a traveling companion? Or was it the fact that each hour seemed to drag on due to exhaustion? She shouldn't be that tired. Rose didn't do nearly as much manual labor on the ranch as she usually did at home. It had basically been a vacation. So why was she so tired? Emotional exhaustion, perhaps?

Lavender picked her up at the airport and the warm hug from her sister felt like a soothing balm on her cracked, weathered heart.

"Oh, sweetie. You look miserable."

Rose arched an eyebrow. "Well, thank you, dear sister. You sure know how to make a girl feel beautiful."

Lavender smiled, properly chastised. "I just mean, I'm sorry you came home alone."

Rose released a deep sigh. She was sorry too. "I guess it's for the best. What did I expect? After all, I'm the one who pushed him to go back home and give his family a chance. I just didn't expect that mean I'd lose my best friend in the process." Her voice cracked with emotion. What was she going to do? The farm would never be the same without Tate and his quirky jokes or their ridiculous wagers. Not only was she losing the future she'd started imagining together, but she was losing the closest friend she'd had for four years.

"It's going to be okay, Rose. It's still Bloom's Farm and you've still got all of us."

"Thanks. I'm sure eventually I'll get over it."

Eventually sounded like a long time away though.

A week later, Rose was still fighting the ingrained habit of stopping by Tate's office for a morning cup of coffee. Her heart rate still increased when someone stepped through the door of the barn, half-expecting it to be him.

It never was.

When she asked her mom if she had heard anything, Laura admitted that Tate had called and officially resigned, effective immediately. Poppy and the kids were living at their farmhouse as much as possible, and Hawthorne and her dad were juggling the produce operation.

Rose was disappointed he hadn't even come back to say goodbye to everyone in person. Even if he had hard feelings toward her, her family had welcomed him in.

But he had his own family now.

23

On the ranch, Tate was finding the familiar rhythm of his teenage summers. Without Rose, he spent his evenings with his family, or frequently, alone with Dad at the house while Travis hit up the local bars.

He had debated the wisdom of taking a trip back to Indiana for weeks. Even after he'd called and talked to Laura Bloom, resigning from his position at Bloom's Farm, he wasn't sure. He felt like Keith and Laura deserved a proper goodbye. Technically, he also had a few things left behind at Miss Ruth's cabin. But it wasn't much, and nothing he couldn't replace.

The biggest hesitation was because he didn't

know what he'd do when he arrived. Beg for his job back? Beg for forgiveness from Rose?

What would that accomplish? He still wanted to be here on Russell Ranch. As he watched his father get weaker, he wanted to step up and be the son who stayed and helped. Tate wanted that relationship with Travis.

Rose had clearly decided where her priorities were, and they didn't leave room for him unless he was at Bloom's Farm. Oh, but he missed her. He'd typed out a dozen text messages and deleted them, unsent.

"It's so good to have you back around, Tate. I don't know what we would have done without you." His brother's words at dinner made him sit up a little straighter and stroked his pride in his decision. It was the right decision, wasn't it?

"It's good to be here. But you would have survived. That's what we always do, isn't it?"

His dad echoed the sentiment. "Travis is right. We need you here." His words were punctuated with a few wheezing coughs, and Tate felt a tug of sympathy, followed by guilt that it had taken him so long to come back. He needed to be here.

"Thanks, Dad."

A week later, Tate was at the front gate, fixing the crooked letters on the Russell Ranch sign when a white truck pulled up, a familiar logo on the side. What was the US Department of Agriculture doing here? They almost never bothered cattle producers. They focused on inspecting the final products at the meat processors.

A man stepped from the front cab and Tate climbed down from the ladder, wiping his hands on a rag from his pocket.

"Can I help you?"

"Wilson Pritchett, USDA enforcement. I'm looking for Steve Russell."

"I'm his son. What's this about?"

"I really need to see the owner of the property."

Tate pressed his lips together. "Follow me up to the main house. Dad's been sick, but I'll see how he is feeling today." He called Travis from his truck on the way back up the drive.

When they were seated around the kitchen table, Travis was noticeably nervous. Tate gave him a questioning look, which his brother ignored.

It was natural to be nervous when the USDA showed up. They had the authority to essentially shut down the ranch, or at least make it impossible to find a buyer for their cattle. But why would they do that? Was there something wrong with the herd?

Steve coughed. "What's this all about?"

The man from the USDA pulled out a manila folder and flipped it open. "It has come to our attention that cattle from this ranch have tested high for residual chemicals."

Tate exhaled a sigh of relief. It wasn't uncommon for trace amounts of antibiotics to occasionally be found in butchered meat. It wasn't allowed either, but it wasn't a shut-down-the-ranch emergency.

"Well, we all know this happens sometimes, through no ill intent," Tate started.

Mr. Pritchett held up a hand. "I'm not talking about one carcass with some antibiotics. So far, we have forty-three carcasses confirmed with DES, the banned growth hormone, traced back to Russell Ranch."

Tate's mouth fell open. He looked at his brother. "What is he talking about, Travis?"

A nervous laugh escaped from Travis. "There must be some mistake."

His brother was no help, and Tate looked to his left. "Dad?"

His father sighed. "There's no point in denying it, Travis."

"You have the right to an attorney. We at the USDA Food Safety Inspection Service do not take the endangerment of human life lightly. The entire herd will be tested, and all affected cattle will be tagged as ineligible for processing."

Travis jumped to his feet. "You can't do that!"

"Sit down, Travis. Are you insane?" Tate's mind was reeling. He knew DES had been banned decades ago. The very idea that his family was using it on purpose for their cattle made him physically sick. He turned back to Travis. "How long?" When his brother ignored him, he demanded again. "How long, Travis?"

Travis hung his head. "The first ones sold last winter."

Tate pressed his fingers into his eyes. "I'm an idiot." He had actually believed that his family was capable of thinking of something other than success. That they cared about him. What a joke. "How could I have been so naïve?"

The USDA officer slid another paper across the table. "To date, the forty-three affected carcasses have been condemned. The evidence has been handed over to the USDA Office of the General Council and the US Attorney. Civil and criminal charges will be brought against all responsible parties."

Travis's face went white. "Criminal charges?"

"In addition to the live property disposition, we are looking at up to 500,000 dollars in fines and up to 10 years' imprisonment."

This was a nightmare.

"It's over. After all these years, I end up losing the ranch in the end." Tate's father hung his head, and Tate almost felt sorry for his old man. Almost.

Mr. Pritchett continued talking, explaining the court date and process as Tate glared at his brother for getting them into this mess.

Finally, the USDA inspector finished.

Tate showed him out to his car. "Mr. Pritchett, I'm Tate Russell. I want to be real with you. Until three weeks ago, I hadn't set foot on this ranch in a decade. I had absolutely nothing to do with the decision of my father and brother to juice the cattle. You have to believe me."

Mr. Pritchett nodded. "I do believe you. Mostly because we've been investigating for a few months and your name has never come up in connection with the ranch. But, Mr. Russell, you're in a tight spot. Your family has made some incredibly poor and dangerous decisions."

"Is there anything I could do, independently, to protect the future of the ranch? Without them, obviously."

The inspector shook his head. "I'm sorry. It will all depend on the outcome of the court case." He tilted his head and looked up, thinking. "Actually, if in the process of judgement, the ranch is foreclosed on, you *could* petition the court for first rights of refusal when the land is sold."

Tate's head was spinning. "That's good information, I really appreciate it."

"Good luck, son. You're going to need it." He shook Mr. Pritchett's hand and turned back to the house.

Tate marched back into the kitchen, the anger rising within him again at the sight of his brother.

"For crying out loud, Travis. What the heck were you thinking?"

Travis whirled around and jabbed a finger into Tate's chest. "You weren't here, Tate. You don't get to judge me. We had to do *something* to save the ranch, and I did what I had to do."

"You could have killed people!" The sentence sounded absurd even coming out of his mouth. He knew it was true though. "Dad, how could you have let him do this?"

His father remained at the table, staring coldly at the papers. "We made a choice to save the ranch. Maybe it was the wrong choice, but it's done."

"*Maybe* it was the wrong choice? Do you even hear yourselves? The man said ten years in prison!" Tate had never been so tempted to put his fist through a wall. Instead, he turned away and went back outside, letting the screen door slam behind him.

24

The familiar gait of her father caught her eye as he walked across the barn. "Hey, Dad. What brings you out in the heat?"

Keith Bloom smiled and looked around. "Good for these old bones to get out of the house. Besides, I wanted to see if you needed any help. This is a lot to take care of."

"For me?" Rose wished she could take the words back as soon as she said them, but there it was. Her father's face fell and he shook his head.

"No, Rosie. For anyone."

She sighed. "I'm sorry, Dad. I didn't mean that the way it sounded."

"How did you mean it?"

Rose weighed her words carefully this time.

"Sometimes I still feel like I'm trying to prove myself to you and Hawthorne. And when you guys come out here to check up on me, it's like you don't trust me." She couldn't look at her father during the confession, so she watched Margie in her pen. "It's been five years, Dad. Isn't that enough?"

"I... I'm sorry, Rosie. I didn't realize you felt that way. We are just trying to help, you know."

"I don't need your help though. You didn't hover over Tate to make sure he planted the tomatoes far enough apart. And you don't look over Mom's shoulder when she's running payroll to make sure everyone gets the right number of hours. But you've never trusted me to do what is needed."

Rose stuffed her hands in the pockets of her coat. "Before your stroke, do you remember what happened?"

Her dad frowned and shook his head. "That whole day is pretty murky."

She turned to her dad and noticed the deep lines on his face and the wispy white hair sneaking out from under his ball cap. "We fought that morning. This same conversation, but worse. I'd been home, working here full-time for a year, but you insisted on a breakdown of everything I'd done each day. You called the vet multiple times instead of trusting my judgement. You trusted Hawthorne to kid the goats instead of me, when you and I both know that he was barely even phoning it in at that point."

She huffed out a breath of air in frustration. "I've worked my entire life learning and working to earn my place as the one in charge. And after five years, you still don't trust me or my judgment." Rose bit down hard on her lower lip, trying not to show how much that lack of trust affected her.

"Rose, I don't come down here because I don't trust you." Her dad's quiet tone settled her racing pulse.

"You don't?" What other explanation could there be?

Keith shook his head and stepped up next to the fence. "I come down here because I love the animals, and I love seeing you with them. Just like I loved watching Poppy manage the crops better than I ever could. I didn't hover over Tate because he's not my son. But seeing you bottle feed a rejected calf, with all the tenderness and strength you were gifted with? It's my favorite thing in the whole world. I love hearing you talk about what you've worked on, because even on a hard day, your eyes light up when you talk about the job."

Rose pressed her lips together and considered his

words. Had she been wrong all this time? What she had interpreted as interference and distrust had really been simple interest? If it was really that simple, then what about the rest of it?

"Why haven't you named me manager?" Her voice cracked on the question. When Hawthorne had taken over as general manager after her dad's stroke, he'd quickly taken on the title and responsibilities associated with it. When Tate was hired on to cover for Poppy after she married Harrison, Tate had been given the title and salary for Operations Manager–Produce. But Rose had no official title, and her salary had remained consistent since she returned to the farm six years ago. She didn't do it for the money, and there was really no prestige in a manager role. It had always been one more thing she pointed to as proof of their underestimation of her.

Now it seemed even more important. Without Tate, all she had was Bloom's Farm and her role here. If they didn't even consider her a manager, what was the point? She'd always been convinced all she needed was her job and her family. But the last few weeks seemed emptier than she ever remembered. If she finally had the approval of her father, would it make a difference?

Keith gave her a confused look. "What do you mean? You're the manager."

She shook her head. "No... No, I'm not. I took on some additional things when you had your stroke, but I didn't get a raise. I didn't get new business cards."

"I'll talk to Hawthorne. I'm sure it just never crossed his mind. You're the manager, Rose. If it isn't you, who would it be?"

She jerked a shoulder. "I don't know. I guess I thought everybody thought it was still you. And I was still just daddy's little girl playing pretend."

Keith dropped an arm around her shoulder. "I'm so proud of everything you do. We'll make sure you get the title—and the salary—you deserve. We never meant to make you feel like you weren't doing a good job."

Rose exhaled deeply and leaned into her father's embrace. "Thanks, Dad. That means more than the title or the money."

Despite her father's words and the reassurance that he trusted her explicitly, Rose was unsatisfied with the result. It was everything she'd ever worked for, but she didn't feel the relief and joy she thought she would. What was missing?

She sent a quick prayer heavenward. Spending

her life pining for Tate wasn't an option, so why did she feel so torn? God had given her a wonderfully blessed life, including a family who loved her unconditionally and a job she treasured. Why wouldn't he take away this longing for a man she couldn't have?

For the first time since leaving Montana, she prayed for Tate. In her anger and frustration, she'd forgotten that her most powerful weapon remained unused. Tate needed wisdom, and though he'd rejected it from her a few weeks ago, God could still move mountains.

Another week passed, and though Rose was still struggling with trusting that God had a plan, she threw herself into her work and continued to pray for peace. While she was laying fresh bedding in the shed for the goats, movement at the edge of the field caught her eye. She shaded her face from the sun with her hand. Was that a cowboy hat? The visitor propped their foot up on the lowest rung of the fence and watched her.

Rose started walking toward the fence and her heart leapt.

A thousand potential greetings warred within her. It's good to see you. I miss you. Please come back. Instead, her question escaped with a gruff tone that in no way resembled the tangle of emotions she felt. "What are you doing here?"

The corner of his mouth twitched, hinting at the crooked smile she so loved to receive. "No beating around the bush, is there Rose?"

"It's good to see you, Cowboy. Hat and all," she added with a nod toward the cowboy hat that replaced his ever-present baseball cap.

His hands went to the rim of his hat, as though he was surprised by its presence. He glanced around the empty field. "Can we talk?"

"I don't know if that's a good idea, Tate."

"Just give me a chance to explain. It's been a doozy of a month. I could really use a friend... and a chance to apologize."

Rose saw the sincerity in his deep brown eyes. He was hurting, and her own curiosity about what he had to say was rising with every minute.

Eventually she nodded. "Okay. I'm about done for the day. Meet me at the house?"

Tate dropped a fist on the top rung of the fence. "All right. I'll be there."

Rose watched him walk away, then leaned against the fence and whispered, "I'm going to need some help here, God." Seeing Tate, even for a minute, felt like ripping open the scab on the wound she'd carefully tucked away and ignored for the last few weeks. But there, within the pulsing ache, was something else. A flicker of hope. He had come, hadn't he? That had to mean something.

She finished her final tasks of the day and walked up to the main house. Tate's white truck sat in the circle drive. Rose entered through the basement and headed straight to her room. She could hear Tate talking upstairs with her parents, but she wasn't ready yet.

After a shower to remove the sweat and grime of her day, Rose carefully braided her hair, leaving half of it tumbling loose around her shoulders. Perhaps it was childish, but Tate could eat his heart out at what he'd given up. Plus, if she was going to have a hard conversation, she was going to feel as confident and self-assured as possible. Which tonight meant not smelling like goats.

She walked upstairs. Her mother saw her first, and her face lit with a smile. "Oh, Rose, you look lovely. We've just been catching up with Tate. Isn't it so nice to see him?"

Tate turned around in his chair then, and she saw his eyes widen. Nailed it.

"That's great, Mom. Tate, are you ready?"

He cleared his throat and nodded. "Yeah. I'm ready."

Tate opened the passenger door of his truck for her, and she climbed up. The warm, dusty smell of the vehicle was reassuring, the same as it had ever been. She glanced at Tate, wishing the same could be said of the two of them.

TATE SET his cowboy hat between them. He turned the ignition, chiding himself to breathe and relax. But his heart was racing and his palms were slick on the steering wheel. "You hungry?"

Rose nodded.

He drove slowly down the drive and off the property. He turned to take them toward Minden. Tate swallowed his nerves and started talking. "First of all, I should apologize."

Rose raised her eyebrows. "For what, exactly?"

"I was so caught up in my own dreams and excitement that I didn't listen to you when you tried to talk to me about it. Travis told me you knew about the DES. And I kept asking myself why you hadn't come to me. Then I realized you had, and I shut you down."

Rose gave him a confused look. "Right. You shut me down. Because you didn't care."

"About you?"

"No, about the hormones."

Tate shook his head with a puzzled frown. "No, Rose. Until the USDA showed up two weeks ago, I had no idea what my dad and brother were up to."

"Of course you did. Travis admitted it, and I heard the two of you talking about it!" She crossed her arms in front of her.

"I promise you, Rose, whatever you heard Travis and I discussing, it wasn't the hormones. I was completely blindsided."

She sat in silence, staring out the window as they passed the fields with tall, tidy rows of corn.

"I was an idiot," he said quietly. "I never should have trusted Travis, but even after ten years, part of me was still holding out hope we could be a family and run the ranch. But they never changed. I'm not sure why I thought they could."

"People do change, Tate." Her hand landed on his shoulder. "I'm sorry they didn't."

He flashed her a tight smile. "Me too. I can't believe they did something so selfish and wrong. I mean, I saw the evidence, so I guess I can believe it. I just don't want to."

"So, now what?"

Tate shook his head. "I don't really know. They'll probably lose the ranch after all the fines. They might even end up in prison."

"Whoa."

"Yep. I'm in the clear since I wasn't even around. I hate to see them punished, but they knew exactly what they were doing. It's hard to feel too bad. I just hate that Russell Ranch will cease to exist from here on out. It's been in our family for seventy years."

"I'm sorry, Tate. I know you love that place. Between your passion for the ranch and the relationship being mended with your family, I really thought you had chosen to ignore the DES. I should have known you would never do that."

"Why did you think I had?"

"For one, Travis told me you knew. Which on its own would never have convinced me. But I heard you talking about not blindly following authority and no one suspecting anything for four years."

Tate tried to remember the conversation she was talking about. They'd been talking about the engagement ring. The very one he still carried with him, in a hopelessly optimistic gesture.

Rose continued her explanation. "It all lined up with what Travis had said. And I still wasn't ready to give up. I was ready to knock some sense into you, but our last conversation... It seemed obvious that you were choosing the ranch and your family and that it was time for me to go home."

"I'm so sorry, Rose. I was convinced that with Bloom's Farm on one side and me with Russell Ranch on the other, you would choose Bloom's Farm." Just like his family had always chosen other things over him. He'd been a fool to color Rose with the same brush. Tate parked in front of B&J Bistro and sighed. "Turns out, it would have been the right choice."

Rose twisted in her seat to look at him. "You had no idea what I would have chosen because you took away my choice, projecting your own insecurities onto me. I thought we were going to figure out the future together."

He hung his head and nodded. "You're right. We should have. I should have."

"I would have chosen you, you know." Rose's statement was quiet, but it shattered the silence in the truck.

His head whipped toward her, only to see her staring at her hands twisted in the purse strap in her lap.

"What?" The word was raw, his throat already burning.

Rose looked up at him, her eyes shiny with tears. "I would have chosen you. Even if that meant Russell Ranch."

"You would have left Bloom's Farm behind? Everything you'd built?"

Rose nodded, and his eyes followed the track of a tear that escaped and ran down her cheek. "I was already thinking about how to talk to Hawthorne about finding someone to take over the livestock and petting zoo here. I would have chosen you. And if Russell Ranch would have been home for you, it would have been home for me." She pressed her eyes closed. "I could see how happy the ranch made you. So much more than running the farm. The livestock on Bloom's Farm would never be enough to keep us both busy. But the ranch? We could have been part-ners, both doing what we loved."

"I'm speechless. I'll never forgive myself for pushing you away like that. I wish... I wish I could go back and do it over. So we could figure out the future together."

"Maybe we still can."

Tate inhaled sharply at her words. He hadn't known what to expect with a visit out here. The only thing he knew was he needed to apologize and tell Rose he'd been wrong. Could she still want to be with him, after everything though?

"Really?" She nodded, and he exhaled a laugh. "There is nothing I'd like more than to dream up a future with you. I'm so sorry."

Rose unbuckled her seatbelt and leaned across the front seat, tucking his cowboy hat on her lap. Instinctively, he wrapped his arm around her and tucked her head against his shoulder. "It's okay. You're here now, right?"

Tate nodded and kissed the crown of her head. "I missed you so much."

"Not nearly as much as I missed you, Cowboy." She sat up and grabbed his cowboy hat, placing it on her head with a grin. His heart leapt at the sight.

"Okay, we definitely have to get you one of those."

Rose laughed. "I don't have much need for one at Bloom's Farm."

Tate's mind was racing. "About that... Let's go inside. There's something I want to talk to you about over dinner."

25

Their plates sat before them, mostly untouched. Rose listened intently as Tate spelled out what he had learned from the USDA official and the lawyer he'd consulted. His eyes never left hers as he finished.

"I don't know if it will work, but there is no one I would rather try to do it with than you."

"Wow." Rose's head was spinning. The idea that they could buy the ranch after everything that had happened was something she'd never considered. "I don't know what to say. How would it even work?"

"I would petition the court for first right of refusal on the ranch once it foreclosed. Assuming the financing works out, the ranch would be mine."

Tate grabbed her hand across the table. "Just to

be clear, I want to be with you more than I want to have the ranch. If you aren't up for this, then just tell me and we'll stay here in Indiana at the farm."

Rose absorbed his words and reveled in the feeling of being loved and chosen. Tate's very offer to stay at Bloom's Farm reaffirmed her own to choose him over the dream she'd held for years. The challenge of rebuilding Russell Ranch from scratch—with integrity—with Tate standing by her side? It was a new dream—one she had never expected but was eager to fully embrace.

Rose shook her head. "The last few weeks at the farm without you have made me realize how meaningless something can be if the right person isn't there with you. If the ranch doesn't work out, which we have to be honest with ourselves and admit is entirely possible, then Bloom's Farm might be the place for us. Or maybe there is another ranch out there needing rescue. But I loved Russell Ranch. And more importantly, I love you."

Tate's smile grew wider. "I love you too, Rose. So much." Tate shifted in his chair and reached into his pocket. "You know that conversation you overheard between me and Travis? Well, I already told you it wasn't about the drugs. But I never told you what it was about."

Rose frowned. "No, I guess you didn't. It doesn't matter though. It was a mistake."

Tate's smile remained unchanged, his eyes twinkling as he slid from the chair. What was he doing?

On one knee in front of her, Tate looked up and spoke quietly. "Rose Marie Bloom, when I told my brother I was putting family first, I was talking about you. When I said I wasn't listening to authority, I was talking about my father and his stubborn refusal to give me this ring." Rose's eyes flew to the ring suddenly visible in Tate's hand.

She gasped. "What on earth?"

Tate reached for her hand. "Rose, while we were at the ranch, I was convinced that you were the only woman for me. After our time apart, I'm even more sure. I don't want to rescue the ranch without you. I don't even want to face tomorrow without you. If you'll have me, I promise to spend the rest of my life proving just how much I love you by putting you second."

She tipped her head with a questioning smile. Did he say second?

He continued, "Above myself. Above the ranch or my work. Above our children someday, I hope. I promise to put God first, so I can lead you well and put you rightly at the top of the rest of the list."

Rose felt like she shouldn't be able to cry anymore, but she felt the tears roll down her cheeks, which were stretched with a smile.

"Rose, will you marry me?"

Unable to speak, she simply nodded and covered her mouth as a laughing sob escaped. Tate grinned and slipped the ring on her finger before she pulled him off his knees and into her arms. Polite applause rang out around them in the small restaurant. Rose wiped her eyes on his shoulder and turned her face to his.

As though he could read her thoughts, Tate pressed his lips to hers and sealed the promises he'd made with a kiss. For a brief moment, she drank in the dark, delicious taste of him and curled her fingers into the hair at the nape of his neck. Then they broke the kiss, and he tightened his embrace before releasing her entirely.

Rose sat back down at the table, suddenly aware of all the eyes on them. She covered her face with her hands, and her shoulders shook with laughter. "We're engaged!"

Tate nodded with amusement. "Yes, at least, I'm pretty sure that's what just happened."

"Oh my word. I can't believe you proposed."

"Hey, don't forget that you said yes."

She laughed. "I'll bet you I'll never forget."

"Only a fool would take that bet. Because I plan to spend my whole life reminding you."

"Do you want to come inside for a bit?" Rose wasn't ready to say goodnight yet.

They walked inside together, hand in hand. Her mom and dad were in their customary places in the living room, a baseball game on the television.

Her mother greeted them with a kind smile. "Did you two have a good night?"

Rose felt her cheeks redden, and her own smile was too powerful to contain. She held up her left hand. "We're engaged!"

Laura Bloom leapt to her feet with a celebratory cheer, scurrying across the living room for a hug. She wrapped Rose in her arms first. "Oh, sweetie. I'm so happy for you. Congratulations!" She turned to Tate. "And you! How dare you call and quit on us? But you're back now. Keith, get over here!"

Rose looked at her dad making his way across the room. His unhurried shuffle was coupled with a broad smile and already open arms. Rose closed the gap and stepped into them. "Congratulations, Rosie."

"Thanks, Dad."

Tate cleared his throat. "Mr. Bloom, I suppose I should have asked permission. I didn't exactly plan on asking tonight."

"And yet, she has a ring..." Thankfully her father's voice held amusement, not condemnation.

"May we have your blessing?" Tate's voice held a hint of trepidation, and Rose lifted her eyes to look at her father.

He looked between the two of them. "I could see how your absence was affecting my little girl over the past few weeks. I know I don't know the whole story, but can you assure me that whatever came between you will never do so again?"

Rose knew her father was only looking after her. He wasn't wrong. Just this morning, he'd tried to talk to her about what was wrong, and she'd insisted it was nothing. How had she been blessed with such an amazing family, while Tate's was the complete opposite?

"I can, sir. I've learned a lot of hard lessons in the past few weeks. And I'll never make the same mistake I did before."

"What mistake was that?"

"I didn't listen to Rose when she was trying to help. I ended up trusting the wrong person because I put my pride ahead of my heart."

Keith wrapped an arm around her mother. "It's not easy to admit your mistakes." His eyes shifted to Rose, "It's also not easy to stand by your partner when they make them. If you two can continue to do that moving forward, you'll be just fine."

The next day, Rose got the attention of everyone at family brunch. "Tate and I have an announcement."

"Don't you think we figured out that he's back and you're together again?" Hawthorne's sarcastic question drew chuckles around the room, and Rose rewarded him with an eye roll.

"Well, yes. And no." At the questioning looks, she pulled the ring out of her jean pocket and slipped it on. "We're engaged."

Daisy's excited shriek made Rose wince. She was instantly engulfed in a hug on two sides as Lavender and Avery made their excitement known.

Daisy made her way over, more slowly with her tiny baby bump leading the way. "I'm so happy for you two. You were great as friends, but you are even better as a couple."

"This is awesome," Hawthorne said through

bites of cinnamon roll. "You guys will be like the next Mom and Dad on the farm. You're not allowed to fire me though."

Rose's smiled slipped. Now wasn't the time, but when would be the right time to tell her entire family that they might leave?

Tate squeezed her hand, "I think your job is safe, Hawthorne."

Brunch continued, and conversations swirled around her about the engagement. Topics shifted to Daisy's baby shower and Andi's plans to move home soon. If they took over the ranch, she was going to miss so many things moving away. Could she build a life fifteen hundred miles away from everything she'd ever known?

Rose stood up and went to refill her coffee cup, then busied herself making a fresh pot. She jumped lightly when a warm hand landed on the small of her back.

"Hey." Tate's deep voice had her wanting to melt into a puddle. "Are you okay?"

She turned around and saw his concerned gaze. "I'm fine."

Tate looked over his shoulder, then tugged her into the laundry room. "Tell me what's wrong."

She leaned into his strong chest and took a deep

breath. "It's hard to realize all that we will miss out on not being around here all the time."

"We don't have to go, Rose. I mean it."

She shook her head. "No, no. I want to. It's just going to be different, you know? But Andi has lived across the country for almost twenty years, and she is still every bit our sister."

Tate ducked down to meet her eyes. "You're sure?"

"Absolutely."

"I love you."

"I love you too."

That brief interaction with him was all she needed, and the tension in her neck and shoulders released. It wouldn't be easy to be so far away, but it would be worth it.

26

*F*our months later, Tate once again drove down the dusty road to his family ranch. This time, he was in his own truck, pulling a trailer packed with wedding gifts and the combined belongings of him and his new bride.

Tate turned and watched Rose gently snore in the passenger seat. He knew without a doubt, he wouldn't be achieving this dream without her. The last few months had been a whirlwind of lawyers and banks and wedding plans.

His brother and father had pled guilty and settled with the USDA to avoid jail time. The resulting fines could only be covered by the USDA foreclosing on the ranch. Thankfully, their prayers had been answered and Tate had been given the chance to make the first offer to buy back the property.

The result was a mountain of debt, but he and Rose were now the proud owner of six thousand acres of the most gorgeous Montana pasture he'd ever seen. Their herd was small, but they'd been allowed to keep any cattle that wouldn't be sold within the twelve months of removing the DES implants.

As they approached the front drive, he reached over and patted Rose on the thigh. "Wake up, beautiful. We're here."

Rose opened her eyes and sat up straighter with a yawn. "How long was I out?"

"You fell asleep just outside of Billings, but I don't mind. You're cute when you snore."

"I do *not* snore!"

Tate chuckled. "Want to bet?"

Rose didn't answer, but her eyes danced with laughter. Tate pulled the truck to a stop at the entrance. The sign over the road greeted them. "Russell Ranch," Rose said proudly as she joined her hand in his.

"You know, I was thinking maybe it was time Russell Ranch found a new identity. What do you say we add another R to that sign and call it Rose Ridge Ranch?"

Rose's eyes widened. "Tate, are you sure? This is your family ranch. Shouldn't it stay Russell Ranch?"

Tate gave a small smile. "It's the land I didn't want to lose. Not the name. The Russell Ranch name will have a bad reputation for a long time after what my family pulled. This is ours now. I think a new name would be a great way to start fresh. What do you think?"

"I think... I think it's perfect, Tate."

He grinned and pulled the truck through the gate and up the gravel drive to their new home. Eight hours later, they collapsed on the front porch swing. They'd been unloading boxes and settling into the house all day. Jimmy, the foreman who had agreed to keep things running in the transition, had stopped by and given them a rundown on the state of things. It wasn't pretty. They had a long road ahead of them.

But sitting there, with Rose tucked against his shoulder, watching the sun sink below the horizon and painting the sky a brilliant reddish-orange, Tate couldn't help but say a prayer of thanks.

ROSE FELT the bed shift as Tate rolled out. She mumbled through the haze of sleep. "I checked them at midnight."

Tate whispered in response. "It's nearly four. I'll just make sure everyone is okay. Go back to sleep, love."

Rose stretched and let out a yawn. "No, I'm coming. As long as you make the coffee."

Twenty minutes later, Rose drank deeply from the thermos of coffee and let out a sigh of satisfaction. The spring calving season was well underway, and these nightly checks were part of the job. At least they could share the responsibility with their farmhands, who were rapidly becoming indispensable.

She handed the coffee to Tate after he opened the gate to the calving lot. Without much discussion, they split up to survey the lot and evaluate the progress. Rose grinned when she spotted a new calf along the left fence line with its mother. She quickly slipped a collar around its neck and recorded the information in her notebook. It was a healthy male and was already standing and nursing. When she finished, her eyes searched the lot for Tate.

Her husband was kneeling beside a heifer across the lot and she quickly walked that way. When she knelt next to Tate, Rose registered the wrinkle of worry across his brow. "Did you notice her last night when you checked?"

Rose pulled out her notes. "She wasn't in active labor at midnight, but her tail was out and she was restless." There was no telling how long the heifer had been in active labor at this point, but it was less than a few hours. "Let me check her." Rose examined the birth canal, saw the tiny feet protruding and retracting with each contraction. "She needs help. Can you grab the chains?"

As Rose and Tate worked together to free the calf, Rose couldn't help but think back to the late nights they'd spent kidding goats at Bloom's Farm. In some ways, that was where their friendship had truly developed. Despite her initial fears that Tate was a threat to her future, it turned out he was the key to it.

Rose never imagined leaving Bloom's Farm and her family legacy. But as Tate cleared the calf's airways and rubbed it down, Rose couldn't imagine being anywhere else—with anyone else. They stayed by the calf and its mother for an hour, a triumphant cheer when the calf stood on its own.

As the first rays of morning sun peaked over the eastern horizon, Rose tucked herself under Tate's arm and leaned into his strong frame. Tate looked down at her with a lazy smile and she tipped her chin up in invitation.

His lips met hers in a slow, gentle kiss. Rose would never tire of the way Tate made her feel.

Adored.

Desired.

Respected.

"I love you, Cowboy," she whispered when they broke the kiss. Tate's dark eyes were flecked with gold in the morning light as they met hers.

"I love you more," he replied.

She gave him a cheeky smile. "Want to bet?"

EPILOGUE

*K*eith Bloom watched through the window, eagerly waiting for Rose and Tate to pull in the drive. The Thanksgiving celebration couldn't start without them. It didn't seem possible that they'd been gone for a year. Admittedly, he and his wife were disappointed when they couldn't make it back for the holidays last year. As much as anyone, he could appreciate how much work there was to be done and the price of being the one responsible. He had spent more than one holiday working on the farm instead of traveling to see extended family.

He and Laura had visited once in the spring, but it had been far too long since he'd seen his youngest daughter and her husband. He'd watched Tate mature before his eyes while he lived at Bloom's Farm, from a hardworking man with something to prove into a God-fearing man striving to live daily for Christ.

When the rental car pulled into the driveway, he called into the kitchen where the rest of the family was gathered. "They're here!"

A stampede of footsteps raced out of the house. Little Henry, just shy of two years old now, looked shell-shocked amid the chaos, and Keith swooped him up. "Should we go see Aunt Rose?"

Rose was already wrapped in hugs from her sisters when he made it outside, her wide smile shining as bright as he ever remembered. Henry fussed to be released and Keith set him down to run free. The initial wave of hugs subsided and he stepped closer. Rose looked different. Older, perhaps, but mostly he sensed a deep-seated contentment.

"Oh, Rosie. It's so good to see you," he said softly as he wrapped his arms around her.

"Thanks, Dad. I've missed you so much."

Keith let her go and took the offered hand from Tate, pulling him in for a hug as well. "Glad you made it."

He stepped back and watched Laura wrap Tate

in a warm hug. She had been the one who hired Tate five years ago. He remembered the conversation they'd had at the time. It had been mostly one-sided, to be fair, since it was shortly after his stroke. But Laura had been sure Tate was exactly what Bloom's Farm needed, and—more importantly—that Bloom's Farm was exactly what Tate needed.

Laura was the biggest blessing in his life, followed closely by the seven wonderful children they'd raised together. When he'd had his stroke, the hardest part hadn't been the struggle to talk, or even the frustrating loss of independence and extreme weakness. It had been knowing that he had become a burden to his beautiful wife.

When he looked at the faces of his daughters, it was impossible not to notice his wife's familiar features. Her hair and smile, yes. But also her kindness and generosity. He couldn't have asked for a better partner to work the farm and raise a family over the last forty years. Looking at Rose and Tate, he knew it would be the same.

Through thick and thin, Rose and Tate would be partners. Now, they were each other's family. Of course, even though they lived 1500 miles away, they were part of the Bloom family too.

~

Laura pulled the green bean casserole out of the oven and ran through her mental list of dishes for Thanksgiving dinner. For the first time in more years than she cared to count, all seven of her children were home. Rose and Tate were visiting, taking a short break from the ranch in Montana. Lily and Josh were here, introducing Maia to her aunt and uncle. The small Guatemalan girl was painfully shy, but Laura's heart nearly exploded each time she saw Lily's hand wrapped in her tiny fingers.

The recent adoption brought her number of grandchildren to five. Magnolia and Henry split their time between the capital and their house on the farm. Lavender was currently in the other room, nursing four-month-old Caleb, their miracle baby after a difficult journey.

Daisy's daughter, Brielle, turned one a few months ago and was currently being passed back and forth between her mother and Andi, Daisy's twin sister. Each time she spotted the other across the room, she reached for them, much to the amusement of the rest of the family. Having Andi home was a special treat, for sure.

Andi was retiring from the Army next summer,

but what she would do after that remained to be seen. Laura had never prayed as hard as she did when Andi had been deployed, a staggering four different times, but lately she'd felt a pull to cover her adventurous daughter in prayer even more.

Andi was coming to a crossroads in her life, and Laura would be there to cheer her on. Admittedly, she was secretly hoping Andi would move back home. More importantly, she hoped Andi would realize true peace. Not that Laura wasn't incredibly proud of everything Andi had faced and accomplished. But her daughter had been working tirelessly for years, striving toward something Laura couldn't identify.

Perhaps this retirement was a chance for Andi to reset and reevaluate. Maybe she would even find love.

ABOUT DANCING WITH DANDELION

They can't agree on anything—except that the job comes first.

Dandelion "Andi" Bloom has sacrificed a lot for her career in the Army. Now that she's retired, playing security guard at Bloom's Farm for high-profile events is a welcome change of pace. That is, until a string of political events means working with a Secret Service detail – including a certain special agent she would have rather left behind in Virginia.

Special Agent Ross McClain takes his job seriously. Even if he has to come to the middle-of-nowhere in Indiana to work events for the Vice-Presidential candidate. On Bloom's Farm, Ross runs into a familiar—and unwelcoming—face. Could this assignment get any worse?

Despite their mutual disdain, Andi and Ross must work together to provide security for the farm and the candidate. As the assignment goes on, it becomes impossible not to clash over every decision —and even harder to deny their growing chemistry.

Dancing with Dandelion is Book 7 in the Bloom Sisters Series. This small town, family saga is full of heartwarming themes, swoony-worthy kisses, and sweet happy endings.

NOTE TO READERS

Thank you for picking up (or downloading!) this book. If you enjoyed it, please consider taking a minute to leave a review or rating. They make a huge difference in the success of a book!

I loved watching Rose and Tate become more-than-friends, and I hope you did, too. It was fun to watch them banter and play, but also have real conversations with apologies and misunderstandings. Plus, I loved seeing Tate grow in his faith and really internalize what it meant to be a Christian

I pray my books encourage you in your faith and through your struggles, whatever they may be.

You can learn more about my upcoming projects at my website: www.taragraceericson.com or by signing up for my newsletter. Just for signing up, you will get a free story!

If you've never read my other books, I'd love for you to read the Main Street Minden Series and dive into the world of Minden, Indiana. Or, read more about the Bloom Family in Hoping for Hawthorne or the other books in the series!

Thank you again for all your support and encouragement.

ACKNOWLEDGMENTS

Above all, to the Lord Almighty. I can only to do this because You give me the words, the strength, and the time. Your faithfulness reaches to the sky.

To my editor, Jessica from BH Writing Services. As usual, this book wouldn't be its best without your insight, encouragement, and friendship. I'm blessed to have you on my team.

To Hannah Jo Abbott and Mandi Blake, for being the best accountability, prayer, and venting partners a girl could ask for.

And to the rest of our Author Circle -- Jess Mastorakos, Elizabeth Maddrey and K Leah. I'm so grateful for each of you and the way we all make each other better.

To Gabbi, for always allowing me to be real.

To my parents, for being a wonderful example of love, faith, and hard work. Especially to my mother, for being my extra set of eyes (and ears) for every story!

Thank you to all my readers, without whose support and encouragement, I would have given up a long time ago.

Special thanks to my beautiful cover models, Deana and Matt for letting me feature you on this book. And to the talented photographer, Emily Kowalski Photography for granting permission to use the image!

And finally, to my husband. I can barely find the words to share how incredibly blessed I feel to have you as my partner. Thank you for your endless patience and encouragement. The way you love, provide for, and lead our family is everything.

Mr. B and Little C; Mommy loves you more than a million words can express.

And Baby L – Welcome to the world, sweet boy. I can't wait to watch you grow.

ABOUT THE AUTHOR

Tara Grace Ericson lives in Missouri with her husband and three sons. She studied engineering and worked as an engineer for many years before embracing her creative side to become a full-time author. Now, she spends her days chasing her boys and writing books when she can.

She loves cooking, crocheting, and reading books by the dozen. Her writing partner is usually her black lab - Ruby - and a good cup of coffee or tea. Tara unashamedly watches Hallmark movies all winter long, even though they are predictable and cheesy. She loves a good "happily ever after" with an engaging love story. That's why Tara focuses on writing clean contemporary romance, with an emphasis on Christian faith and living. She wants to encourage her readers with stories of men and women who live out their faith in tough situations.

BOOKS BY TARA GRACE ERICSON

The Main Street Minden Series

Falling on Main Street

Winter Wishes

Spring Fever

Summer to Remember

Kissing in the Kitchen: A Main Street Minden Novella

The Bloom Sisters Series

Hoping for Hawthorne - A Bloom Family Novella

A Date for Daisy

Poppy's Proposal

Lavender and Lace

Longing for Lily

Resisting Rose